Huckleberry Henry

The
Lost Journal

Volume One

As Recounted by
Phil Hudson

Publishing Services by BookCrafters
Parker, Colorado.
www.bookcrafters.net

Table of Contents

Introduction

This anthology of nearly five hundred anecdotes in two volumes is an accurate annotation of entries that were taken from the pages of Huckleberry Henry's personal journal. It was found meticulously wrapped in buckskin and securely tied with leather thongs, tucked inside a rough-hewn cedar chest, that had, in turn, been carefully deposited by Henry in a small cavity in the rock beneath a wide granite overhang high above Lion Creek. There, Henry had made certain that it would remain protected from the elements as well as from woodland creatures and creepy crawlies. Subsequently, he left tantalizing hints relating to the whereabouts of the journal. It was these clues, gleaned by the author during many summers tramping in the woods along the Selkirk Crest, that led him to its discovery. It seems clear that the journal had been preserved by the Hand of the Almighty to give those of us who believe in the Strange Tale of Huckleberry Henry further insight into his every-day activities. The circumstances of his life in the woods above Priest Lake, Idaho were unique; nevertheless, each of us can learn valuable lessons from his experiences that can be applied to our own benefit.

Dedication

This dedication to Huckleberry Henry acknowledges his resourcefulness in the face of challenging circumstances, and pays homage to his ingenuity in maximizing available resources, even when they have been meager. His expertise in wilderness survival when presented with daunting obstacles has been impressive, and his perseverance when others would have given up hope, and his optimism after repeated failures, is rousing. His gratitude to divine provenance, his philosophical acceptance of his fate, his undaunted courage, his humility, and his confidence when there has been little to hope for, is stirring. His cheerfulness on even the darkest winter nights is without peer, as has been his refusal to accept the withering judgment of others when he has been unfairly judged a lost soul. His ability to find and listen to his internal chronometer and to synchronize it with the majestic clockwork of the heavens is unprecedented, as is his ability to be at-one with the wind and the waves and the ocean of thought. The transformation of his consciousness and self-awareness into spiritual solidarity relating to the divine origin of all of God's creatures both great and small, has led to the ignition of a fire in his bones that has driven him to burst free of the limitations of conventional lowlanders. He has surrendered himself to the providential God of Nature with a serenity that allows him to accept the things he cannot change, to have the courage to change the things he can, and to possess the wisdom to know the difference.

About Huckleberry Henry

The legendary tales surrounding the exploits of Huckleberry Henry are similar to those of Liver Eating Johnson, whose own introduction deserves a re-telling: "His name was Jeremiah Johnson. They say he wanted to be a mountain man. The story goes that he was of a proper wit and an adventurous spirit that was suited to the mountains. Nobody knows where abouts he come from, and it don't seem to matter much. He was a young man and ghostly stories about the mountains didn't scare him none. He was lookin' for a 50 caliber Hawkin rifle. He settled for a 30 caliber, but damn, it was a genuine Hawkin, and you couldn't go no better. Bought him a good horse, traps and other truck that went with being a mountain man and said goodbye to whatever life was down below. This here's his story." The discovery of The Lost Journal of Huckleberry Henry has introduced a new audience to similar adventures.

Acknowledgement

These excerpts from Henrys Journal paint a portrait that illustrates the links between a firm grasp of wilderness survival, a comprehensive knowledge of local history, a self-effacing appreciation of nature, and practical insight relating to their impact on philosophy, religion, and provident living. His musings illustrate his resourcefulness and exemplary hands-on expertise in the face of challenging circumstances. He has exhibited noteworthy ingenuity as he has exploited meager options. When presented with daunting obstacles, his abundant capabilities have been empowering. His perseverance when others would have given up hope has been stirring, and has contributed to a wider view that others are only now beginning to emulate as they begin to experience for themselves its liberting nature. His buoyancy after repeated failures and his gratitude to Divine Providence for the talents he has, have been remarkable. His philosophical acceptance of the things he lacks, and his undaunted courage during his voyage of discovery, have been inspiring.

His humility when confronted by the awesome power of Mother Nature has been unpretentiously modest and self-effacing. His confidence when there has been little to hope for illustrates his unbounded optimism. His cheerfulness on even the darkest and coldest winter nights has been genial and contagious. He has been resolute in his refusal to accept the critical judgment of others, even when it has been withering. His ability to nurture his moral compass, and to synchronize his internal chronometer with the majestic clockwork of the heavens, has been dogged and determined, and his capacity to be at-one with the ocean of thought adjacent to the evolving shoreline of Priest Lake, Idaho has been inexhaustible.

Journal Entries

Annotated by Phil Hudson

William Wordsworth may have had Huckleberry Henry in mind, when he mused that "heaven lies about us in our infancy. Shades of the prison house begin to close upon the growing boy, but he beholds the light and whence it flows. He sees it in his joy. The youth, who daily farther from the east must travel, still is nature's priest, and by the vision splendid, is on his way attended. At length, the man perceives it die away, and fade into the light of common day." In a sense, Henry has done just that as he has faded into the light of common day up on the Selkirk Crest. And yet, he would argue that there is nothing ordinary about living in the mountains, learning to adapt, and accommodating the quirky personality of Mother Nature. As this volume will amply illustrate, Henry's journey has been a wonderful learning experience, and he hopes that by reading about his adventures, some of his practical education will rub off on you. If you can supplement that by learning a few life lessons on your own along the way, all the better. Henry's efforts will not have been in vain, and he will consider his small sacrifices a worthy price to pay for your enlightenment.

Living in the woods as he does, Huckleberry Henry makes sure he always has a stash of dry kindling, for it can spell the difference between spending a warm night beside a crackling fire or shivering in the cold, impatiently waiting for the first rays of the Sun to break through a frigid dawn's early light. Having a roof over his head is not always an option for Henry, and if he doesn't have a torch, blindly boondocking back to his cabin at night is unwise, given that wolves, bears, cougars, and other diurnal predators will also frequently hunt between sunset and sunrise.

Henry has discovered that the rain falls on both the just and the unjust, and in the early spring at Priest Lake, when it rains it pours. So, keeping himself and his clothing dry, as well as his gear, is a high priority. But his socks aren't the only things to which he turns his attention. He also makes sure to protect his gunpowder. Many times, when everything is on the line, Henry's dry powder has spelled the difference between having a meal or going hungry or making it back to his cabin for a cup of hot cocoa and a meat pie instead of becoming dinner for the equally hungry denizens of the forest.

Huckleberry Henry has learned many hard lessons, and among them is this: You may not always be able to stay dry during a rainy spring. It is only because of April showers that Henry has been blessed with May flowers. He hopes and prays for sunny weather but doesn't forget to carry an umbrella. He knows that unrelenting sunshine is more prevalent in the Sahara than in the Selkirks, except maybe in August, when North Idaho gives North Africa a run for its money. Henry is resigned to the fact that if he wants to enjoy a bountiful harvest in the summer, he is going to have to endure soggy weather in the spring. That is something to which lowlanders have equally resigned themselves, as they deal with mud. The germination and blooming of springtime wildflowers are nurtured by showers that also create a lot of puddles. Henry enjoys splashing about in them as much as any other kid at heart, but when he does, he is soberly reminded of that earlier stated rule about keeping his socks and gunpowder dry!

Huckleberry Henry spends the dog days of summer at his cabin on the far side of No Telley Basin, just below Five Mile Ridge, in the shade of a grove of ancient western red cedar that were ignored by the sawyers who cut down the old growth white pine forests in the Idaho Panhandle in the heyday of logging during the early years of the Twentieth Century. It is on his stoop that he has learned to appreciate the vibrantly real and natural beauty of the north country. As he looks to the sun-dappled outlines of Green Bonnet, Mollies' and Phoebe's Tips, and Trapper Peak, he is reminded that, unlike so many lowlanders, he mustn't allow himself to be strangled by illusions of reality, or by the profane baubles of the world whose opacity would obstruct his ability to see what is really out there. Henry tries hard not to judge those folks down below, though. Especially in early spring, March can be a green, yet muddy month. Some like it, he has supposed, farmers mostly.

One of Huckleberry Henrys' reference points when bushwhacking in the Selkirks is Five Mile Ridge. Its exact location isn't a secret, but as many day hikers have discovered, it's extremely hard to pinpoint when dead reckoning, because it's easily five miles from their last pinpointed location and far from where they think it should be. To make matters worse, once the ridge has been located, it's uphill by the four cardinal points of the compass all the way to the Crest, traversing some of the most difficult terrain in the Selkirks to put the most determined hiker within shouting distance of of the Basin.

Henry has quickly learned that it's unwise to seek shelter under the largest tree he can find when he is caught in an autumn thunderstorm and is exposed to the fiery elements of Nature. They say that lightning doesn't strike twice in the same spot, but tell that to the volunteers who staff the towers atop Sundance and Lookout Mountains. What appears at first glance to be shelter, without appreciating the bigger picture, could be a death-trap. In the U.S., an average of 27 people are killed and 247 are injured by lightning every year, so the chance of being one of them is less than one in a million, but ask Henry if that makes him feel more comfortable when he is scrambling down an exposed ridge high up in the Selkirks during a violent thunderstorm.

It may sound silly to state this rule, but it hasn't taken Henry long to learn that If he wants to stay warm in the winter, he will need to build, and maintain, a cozy fire. He has learned that proper prior planning will prevent poor performance. The last situation that he wants to find himself in, is that of fumbling with ungloved hands and frozen fingers to strike a match and put it to soggy kindling, when he desperately needs to warm himself before a crackling fire in cold weather. His skill in igniting a blaze can spell the difference between life and death, or at least between spending a comfortable night in the woods or suffering in silent misery until morning's first light.

Henry hadn't been in the woods for very long before he realized how important it is to "read" the weather report before heading out for the day. He has become a pretty good judge of the signs provided by Mother Nature. He doesn't have access to the five o'clock news, but he gets all the meteorological information he will need by observing shifts in the temperature, the direction and intensity of the wind, the presence or absence of clouds and their type and abundance, as well as the behavior of the animals he encounters in the forest. He has a healthy respect for these signs, and knows that in the Panhandle, the weather can be fickle and turn on a dime. Henry lives by the maxim that "there's no time like the present, and no present like time, and fair weather can be over in the space of a rhyme." (Georgia Byng). It can be colder than witch's breath one minute, and the next, it can be hotter than chili peppers on the Fourth of July.

Air pressure can be an indication of a change in the weather, even without access to a barometer. When the air is heavy and burdensome, or when Henry and the animals he observes in the woods are lethargic, he is alerted to the low pressure of an approaching storm front. On the other hand, when he feels energetic, and when the air seems crisp and light, he looks forward with confidence to heaven in his soul, freshness in his heart, and clear skies in his future, that accompany high pressure.

It has been on both bluebird days and during stormy weather within the sometimes-turbulent borders of the Selkirks that Huckleberry Henry has discovered the tools of perspective and context, that he might better understand and interact with Nature, while the terrestrial and metaphysical jewels of light and truth are scattered about to provide counterpoint for clarity. These have endowed him with the ability to perceive the unseen world within which he has been enveloped, including many wonders in the heavens and celestial glories that can only be discerned when his Creator, working in tandem with Mother Nature, opens his eyes, that he might see.

During these moments of clarity, Henry pauses to give thanks for the bounty of the wilderness. He is particularly sensitive to the circle of life that circumscribes all of Nature, and when he has found it necessary to kill game in order to sustain his own life, over the body of the beast he recites the words of Chingachgook, the last of the Mohicans, who, kneeling before a stag that he had just brought down with his Pennsylvania Long Rife, expressed his sorrow for having been forced to kill his brother, the elk. To the Great Spirit, he acknowledged its speed and celebrated its strength; he honored its courage and sacrifice, and lastly, he asked its forgiveness.

As Henry has fine-tuned his hunting skills, he has observed that game animals can tell when a winter storm is approaching well before it arrives. He notices that they will eat energetically a day or so beforehand, because they know that food will be hard to find once snow has blanketed the ground. Anticipating the heightened activity of deer, moose, and elk, Henry tries to be in the woods just before the storm hits. If he waits too long, and only goes out on a hunt with the arrival of the front, the animals will most likely have already bedded down. Henry doesn't have access to Boone & Crockett Club records that would have confirmed his own observations, but their data demonstrates that over 90 percent of trophy deer are taken when there is no rain or snow falling, typically with a rising or high barometer, and that 85 percent of record bucks are harvested when winds are 5 mph or less. Henry has also discovered that he is most successful as a hunter if he goes back into the woods the minute the storm has broken, since the game he is seeking will be hungry and anxious to leave their bedding areas to look for browse.

Huckleberry Henry has also found that insects respond to air pressure, that ants are busier and move faster when the barometer is high but are lazy and sluggish when it's low. Birds fly closer to the ground in the face of an approaching storm, and clover closes up when rain is imminent. Spiders often abandon their webs and move onto the walls of his cabin with impending bad weather, and a simple observation like seeing smoke that has a harder time rising through his chimney indicates the presence of a low-pressure system, with possible rain in store. A halo around the moon, created when light shines through moisture-laden cirrostratus clouds, often signals the approach of a warm front with possible precipitation. Henry is familiar with the saying: "Red sky at night is a sailor's delight." Many times, he has witnessed a red or pink sunset, caused by dust in the dry, clean air, suggesting fair weather, since most systems, including those at Priest Lake, approach from the west or southwest.

Henry has learned that environmental signs don't just warn of bad weather, though. They can also help to predict fair skies. Nights that are clear with frost, or heavy dew or fog in the morning, are harbingers of good weather. A steady wind is also typical of stable weather, while swirling air and gusty breezes suggest the changeable weather of an approaching front. These signs are variations on the cautionary farewell Henry and other Mountain Men give to each other, to watch their top knot!

Huckleberry Henry may also be aware of the Coriolis Effect, a phenomenon of weather patterns that are created by the rotation of the Earth. In the Northern Hemisphere, storms generally swirl counterclockwise, and yet, many times Henry has witnessed their progression as they have moved from the south along the mountains west of the lake, only to pinwheel around in a clockwise direction within the narrow confines of the Upper Priest Lake Basin, and then to come roaring down out of the north between Ploughboy and Lookout Mountains to release ferocious quantities of energy when hitting the main body of the lake between Mosquito Bay and Beaver Creek Campground.

Fortune has smiled upon Huckleberry Henry, for he has been meticulously groomed to meet his destiny. Winston Churchill argued that there is a little bit of Henry in each of us, when he described the character of our favorite solitary mountain man. He declared: "To each of us, there comes in our lifetime an occasion when we are figuratively tapped on the shoulder and offered a chance to do a very special thing, unique to ourselves and fitted to our talents. What a tragedy if that moment finds us unprepared or unqualified for that which could have been our finest hour." Huckleberry Henry's Lost Journal attests to how well he has been prepared and has become qualified to meet his destiny head-on.

It may be only a matter of time before the Wigwams is renamed in honor of Huckleberry Henry. There is precedent for doing so. In 1951, Looking Glass Mountain, halfway between Coolin and Sandpoint, was renamed Gisborne Mountain after Harry Gisborne, who had been the nation's leading fire research specialist. (Speaking of renaming things, the town of Sagle, Idaho, near Sandpoint, was originally named Eagle. But it was discovered that Idaho already had a town named Eagle, so the town fathers economically substituted an "S" for the "E", and Sagle was born.) As for Gisborne, he had spent almost 30 years at the Priest River Experimental Forest Research Station. The Forest Service considered him the "first true specialist in forest fire research in the nation." A lookout on Gisborne Mountain, built in 1958, is staffed in the summer, and is on the National Historic Lookout Register. At age 56, Gisborne died on the job in 1949 while inspecting the site of a recent fire in Montana. At the time, Gisborne said to a ranger accompanying him: "Here's a nice rock to sit on and watch the river. I made it good. My legs might ache a little tomorrow, though." He never made it off that rock, but in 1951, just a few miles north of the station where he had devoted so many years of his life, a plaque with his name on it was placed on the summit of Gisborne Mountain, that had been renamed in his honor.

Parallels between Gisborne and Huckleberry Henry are revealed in the journal of the latter. Henry recorded that he had also found a big rock at the top of the Wigwams a few days after he had initially lost his way in the woods while out picking huckleberries. He had sat down and said to himself: "Here's a nice rock to sit on where I can try to orient myself. I've made it three days now. Those switchbacks up from the parking lot were tough, and my legs might ache a little tomorrow. But I think I'll be okay." And the rest, as they say, is history.

After his metamorphosis up on the Wigwams, it didn't take long for Henry to learn from the Woodland Elves that he could participate in their nighttime activities. From the start, he was eager to join in as they created trails of jewels on the beaches along Southshores at Huckleberry Bay. Their mission, he has found, is to illuminate the universally accessible pathway to enlightenment. This, Henry has discovered, will lead to broad boulevards flooded by sunlight, paved with cobblestones that glint of gold, caressed by soothing breezes, and lined with huckleberry bushes laden with delicious fruit. Some things, Henry would argue as he combs the glitter from his hair after an evening with the Elves, are easier to experience from the perspective of isolation in the woods, far from the madding crowd.

It doesn't take much to get Huckleberry Henry's full attention when the hairs on the back of his neck stand up straight. There is a certain sixth sense that experienced woodsmen learn to respect when they are boondocking in the backcountry or bushwhacking through dense thickets in unfamiliar terrain. The pupils of their darting eyes constrict, and their pulse rates quicken. Their breathing gets heavier, their mouths become dry, and their trigger fingers twitch. There are potential perils and pitfalls too numerous to mention, and if Henry fails to take notice of each detail, and to instantly act upon every subtle warning sign, he will be doomed to make costly mistakes, and to repeat them with frustrating regularity, but only if Nature benevolently gives him a second chance to make a good first impression in the woods.

As Huckleberry Henry moves about in the backcountry, he makes a mental note of everything he sees. Deer trails crisscross through thickets, suggesting that many animals regularly take those paths. Those he follows lead to refuge cover and feeding areas. In the late fall, he looks for white oak (the Oregon white oak, or Garry oak). These trees are among the hardiest in Idaho, growing in almost any type of soil and thriving in both extreme heat and bitter cold. Their acorns are like candy to deer, who often come at both dawn and dusk to feed. Other deer favorites are strawberries, blueberries, raspberries, chokeberries, and huckleberries. Near these patches, Henry looks for intersecting trails, or convergence points, where he has the chance to see animals approaching from different directions.

During the rut from September thru November, which is the breeding season for moose, elk, and deer, Henry has observed small trees with their bark rubbed off at knee height. The animals make these rubs to mark their territory and to remove velvet from their antlers. He also keeps a sharp eye out for scrapes on low hanging branches, where they have also urinated and left their scent. He has trained himself to notice anything that increases his chances of having venison backstrap, roast, steak, or stew, moose brisket, shank, short loin, hip flank, chuck, and rib sirloin, or elk tenderloin, prime rib, sirloin butt, or top round for dinner.

In the years since his inexplicable banishment to the wilderness above Priest Lake, Huckleberry Henry has somehow avoided the fate of Ebenezer Scrooge. Unlike that old curmudgeon, Henry loves Christmas, even though his perpetual wish to be home for the holidays remains unfulfilled. Scrooge had become cold hearted. He was a miser and the embodiment of despair, sadness, and death. His life was as a dark and lonely winter. As Dickens put it: "The cold within him froze his old features, nipped his pointed nose, made his eyes red, his thin lips blue, and spoke out shrewdly in his grating voice. He was a squeezing, wrenching, grasping, scraping, clutching, covetous old sinner!" He had been worn down by endless waves beating upon his pinched heart. In stark contrast, Henry has somehow managed to escape a similar fate, as evidenced by the hopeful tone of his Lost Journal that optimistically anticipates his own, similar, redemption.

Huckleberry Henry has wandered the length and breadth of Priest Lake's 80-mile shoreline. He has fished the mouths of Upper Priest River and Deadman Creek, that drain into the Upper Lake, Caribou Creek, that drains into the Thoroughfare, Lion Creek, Two Mouth Creek, Indian Creek, Horton Creek, Hunt Creek, and Soldier Creek, that drain into the east side of Priest Lake, as well as Beaver Creek, Granite Creek, Kalispell Creek, Lamb Creek, and Reeder Creek, that drain into the west side of the lake. Minor tributaries flowing into Priest Lake, that have provided Henry with limits of Kokanee, Bull Trout, and Small-mouth Bass, include Binarch Creek, Bottle Creek, Chase Creek, Cougar Creek, Finton Creek, Goblin Creek, Squaw Creek, Tango Creek, and Tepee Creek.

While more than 20 of these creeks feed into Priest Lake, the only outflow through the terminal moraine left at the end of the last Ice Age is at Outlet Bay, where the 44-mile-long Priest River begins its meandering journey to the Pend Oreille River. Originally built in 1950, the first Priest Lake Dam was later replaced by a concrete gravity dam, also known as a "gravity arch dam," a freshwater retaining concrete structure that has a wider base than the top-section. The dam was renovated in 1978. It is used for recreational control of the summer pool level of Priest Lake, and to regulate the release of water for hydroelectric power generation far downstream. The lake level is highly dependent upon environmental conditions such as winter snowpack, the frequency and amount of rainfall throughout the year, and regional drought. Priest Lake Dam is owned and operated by the Idaho Department of Water Resources, but Henry would like to believe that it exists to enhance the enjoyment of Idaho's Crown Jewel by his four-legged friends and neighbors.

Relying upon a drainage basin of nearly a thousand square miles, the average discharge of water from the lake is 1,732 cubic feet per second. A few miles downstream from the dam is McAbee Falls, a minor set of rapids with a vertical drop of only one or two feet over a run of about 50 feet. Regardless, Henry enjoys visiting the falls at the end of a hot summer day. This is when the locals have gathered their beach towels and chilly bins and have returned to the town of Priest River, leaving the rapids for Henry to enjoy in solitude. Occasionally, on his walk back to No Telley Basin, he stops at Chase Lake, which, at 174 acres, is just a fraction of Priest's 26,000 acres. Then, he works his way up Lost Creek, and traverses Horton Ridge before sighting Five Mile Ridge and the trail to No Telley, not far from the base of Mount Roothaan.

When walking along Lion Creek, Two-Mouth Creek, Indian Creek, Horton Creek, Hunt Creek, and Soldier Creek, Huckleberry Henry keeps a sharp eye out for beaver, that had been a fur-trapping staple of the Mountain Man economy in the early days on the western frontier. Before European settlement of North America, the beaver population is estimated to have been between 60 and 400 million, but it was decimated by the appetite of Europeans for fashion. The number of beaver has since rebounded to between 6 and 12 million. Beavers are the largest North American rodents, and they gnaw down trees for both food and construction of their dams. Particularly on the North Fork of Indian Creek, Henry has witnessed first-hand the evidence that beavers are the animals most responsible for environmental change (after humans), establishing wetlands and stimulating biodiversity. Henry has often thought that foresters on Idaho's Endowment Lands, accustomed to a slash and burn style of logging, could learn a lesson or two from the beavers' management of the forest.

Some animals work from the inside of trees, instead of from the outside, as beavers do. Bark beetles bore deep into the trunks to ingest the yummy xylem and phloem found there. Hardly a day passes in the forest without Henry hearing the rat-a-tat-tat of sapsuckers, downy woodpeckers, and northern flickers, on the hunt for insects that have burrowed into the wood. Once they find a beetle, they use their long tongues to scoop them out of the hole. Afterward, the bird's tongues retract around their brains to cushion the shock that is sure to surround the resumption of head-banging.

Henry often watches in fascination as woodpeckers perch on the sides of trees with their tail feathers spread out across the bark for stabilization. The forces of pecking are distributed down through the body of the bird, out the tail, and into the trunk, in an efficient dispersal of energy. The spongy bone of the woodpecker's head is the avian equivalent of a football helmet. They also have very little cerebrospinal fluid surrounding their brains, so there's less chance of their grey matter being transformed into frothy mush during furious pecking. Additionally, they enjoy the biological equivalent of "goggles", to keep flying wood chips out of their eyes. All these adaptations absorb up to 99.7% of the shock of "pecking." When Henry tires while swinging an axe at his cabin, and his hands go numb from splitting firewood, he remembers the relentless focused energy of the woodpeckers and envies their efficiency.

As he tramps through the woods, Huckleberry Henry notices many trees with numerous holes in the trunk. In the spring, to make their nests, woodpeckers bore these holes deep into the trees to create cozy little apartments. Sometimes, and likely without the little woodpecker's consent, these are repurposed as living quarters for barn owls, screech owls, snowy owls, northern hawk owls, pygmy owls, and burrowing owls, which are a few of the 14 colorful species found throughout the Idaho Panhandle.

The quiet water of Priest Lake stands in sharp contrast to the insistent rat-a-tat-tat of the woodpeckers. As Henry gazes out across its mirrored surface, he is mesmerized beneath an evening sky that steals his imagination. The stars in the heavens are wrapped in a fiery red blanket of clouds that merges with the outline of the Selkirk Crest. In the whispering wind, Henry can distinctly hear the voice of God reassuring him that his world is brimming over with unlimited possibilities.

Huckleberry Henry has become an expert at foraging for food in the wild. He has learned to look for those berries that are good sources of carbohydrates, fiber, and vitamins. The ones with tightly packed clusters, like raspberries and mulberries, are edible. Blue, black, and purple berries are around 90% edible, orange and red berries are about 50% edible, and green, white, and yellow berries are only about 10% edible. Henry always conducts a test when he is unsure about whether to pop a plump berry that seems to be bursting with juice into his mouth. He always remembers the maxim that everything in the woods is edible - at least once.

The damp forest floor of the Idaho Panhandle that is covered by sphagnum and other woodland litter is ideal mushroom hunting grounds, and there are several species that are easy to identify and delicious to eat. At higher elevations, Henry is likely to find morels. In lowland wooded areas and around the lake, chanterelles, porcini, giant puffball, lobster, and oyster mushrooms grow in abundance. Other popular varieties that Henry uses in salads and sauces are chicken mushrooms, shaggy mane, and boletes.

If Henry stumbles upon a plant with which he is unfamiliar, he begins by separating out the leaves, stems, buds, berries, flowers, and roots. He focuses on just one of these at a time, giving it a good smell. If it has an unpleasant odor that is particularly strong, it's a sign that the plant might be poisonous. Then, he does a basic edibility test which can be a tedious process, because he takes care to repeat the steps with each part, since certain plants have both edible and inedible portions. The reason Henry invests so much time and energy in the edibility test is because he knows that trusted wild plants can provide him with most of his nutritional needs, and when combined with wild-caught meat and fish, he will enjoy a healthy and varied diet. The most important thing he remembers, however, is that if he remains unsure what the plant is, he doesn't eat it!

Henry looks for the most common traits of poisonous plants. He rules out most mushrooms, and plants with sap that is milky or discolored, that have spines, thorns, or fine hairs, a soapy or bitter taste, or have umbrella-shaped flower clusters and waxy leaves. He steers clear of plants that he cannot identify with certainty but look like parsnip, dill, carrot, or parsley, plants with an almond-like scent in the leaves and woody parts, plants with grain heads that have black, purple, or pink spurs, or a three-leaf growth pattern. When Henry finds himself in a survival situation and isn't sure whether a plant he has found is toxic, he does a skin test by taking a piece of a plant he is considering eating and rubbing it on his inner forearm or outer lip. If he experiences no reaction in 15 minutes, he then does a taste test on the same part of the plant and waits 5 minutes. If there is no taste of bitterness, no soapy flavor, and no numbness on his lips or in his mouth, he takes a teaspoon of the same part of the plant and chews it for 5 minutes, regularly spitting out the excess saliva. He then swallows the fiber and waits 8 hours. In the absence of a reaction, he repeats the process, and waits another 8 hours. If he still experiences no symptoms, he makes a mental note, and considers that part of the plant safe to eat. It's an exhaustive process, but it is far better than the alternative of ingesting a plant that would give him a tummy ache, stimulate nausea, induce an allergic reaction, or worse yet, bring him to death's doorstep.

Henry has always been cautious when it comes to foraging for plant-based food in the wild. He finds that some berries are edible, while their stems and bark are poisonous (such as elderberries). He has discovered that milky sap will often trigger skin irritations or other strong allergic reactions. Fine hairs and spines are another red flag. Umbrella-shaped flower clusters generally are toxic, as are plants with waxy leaves. Mushrooms (like morels, or chanterelle mushrooms) can be a delicacy, but in general, Henry is quite cautious when dealing with fungi that grows on trees or on the ground. He has quickly become familiar with the more common poisonous plants, like rhubarb leaves. Poison oak, sumac, and ivy are easy for Henry to spot, but fortunately, they are relatively uncommon in North Idaho. The three leaves of poison ivy all have pointed tips, with edges that can be either serrated or smooth, but typically look glossy with the middle leaf being the longest. Poison ivy is reddish in the fall, while green to yellow the remainder of the year. Their shiny leaves contain a chemical called urushiol, an oil that causes contact dermatitis. (He takes care to avoid using the leaves of poison ivy to satisfy his personal hygiene needs when in the woods!)

Henry uses the leaves, stems, flowers, pollen, and roots of cattail for wilderness salad, in soup and stew, as a flour, and as a poultice; for baskets and mats, as a torch, and as stuffing for pillows, mattresses, and moccasins. Dandelion makes a delicious and nutritious salad or tea. Elderberry (flower and berries only) is easily transformed into a jam, jelly, or wine, and is useful as a therapy for flu. The spicy taste of garlic mustard adds zest to Henry's sometimes monotonous fare. The seeds of milk thistle and stinging nettle provide a good coffee substitute, and raspberry is rich in antioxidants and makes an elegant pie filling. As a tea, rose hips is high in Vitamin A, B6, C, and in calcium, magnesium, and iron. Henry uses wild carrot (Queen Anne's Lace) in soup, stews, salads, and tea, but he always confirms the plant is wild carrot, and not poison hemlock or fool's parsley, which look very much the same. Poison hemlock and fool's parsley smell bad, and poison hemlock also has a smooth, hairless stem. It can be deadly, so he doesn't eat the plant if he is unsure if it truly is wild carrot.

Huckleberry Henry judges himself fortunate to have created a treasury of reminiscences at Priest Lake. He knows all too well that "the life given us by nature can be short. But the memory of a life well spent is eternal." (Cicero). Contemporary prose illustrates a principle that has guided Henry's life ever since he was lost in the woods: "My father focuses heart-gripping flashes across the wall screen. Family slides. I am small, my brother is smaller, and my sister is smallest. Days now dead re-open like old storybooks from memory's heaped box. Pulling out pictures of cooking in Grandfather's Dutch oven; playing cheetah in our backyard monkey-jungle; being beautifully Easter-bested with my coat buttoned wrong; hugging a mommy minus grey hair. Soberly, I think of the Fashioner of the Universe, Who someday shall open my mind, and flash reeling remembering of every day's minute across my soul, across the heavens, and kindly ask me to narrate." (Lora Lyn Stucker).

Henry prefers snowshoes for mobility in the winter, but he has also tried cross country skiing. It helps that there are 5 miles of groomed trails on the east side of the lake, 6 miles to the south at Coolin Mountain, and another 10 miles at Hanna Flats and Rocky Point on the west. But the real bonus for Henry, if he is going in the general direction of one of the more than 400 miles of groomed snowmobiling tracks, is not having to break his own trail through deep snow. He has followed some of these up into the Selkirks to elevations pushing 7,000 feet. He likes to make first tracks before dawn, and many snowmobilers, snowbikers, cross country skiers, and snowshoers have reported finding the footprint evidence of his passing on the freshly groomed trails.

In 1809, near present-day Hope, Idaho, David Thompson established a North West Company trading post on Lake Pend Oreille. He didn't have the luxury of snowmobile trail groomers or networks of established tracks through the endless wilderness. A voyageur des bois in his party is believed to have given the lake its name. The words are French for "earloop" or "hangs from ears" derived from the custom of members of the Kalispell Tribe to wear dangling shell or bone earrings. Thompson, who was an explorer, cartographer, and fur trader, mentioned in a journal entry "a point of sand" on the spot that is now the center of the community of Sandpoint, Idaho. The town, that lies nestled among fir trees along the northern shore of Lake Pend Oreille, is somewhere between 15 and 25 miles as the crow flies from No Telley Basin. Henry has made the trek over the Selkirks many times, even in winter, following the snowmobiling trail that leads all the way from Coolin. He will often stop for lunch near 6,400-foot-tall Schweitzer Mountain to watch the skiers descending the slopes.

Huckleberry Henry has carved out a good life in the wilderness. He is old enough to remember the crooner, who sang: "And now, the end is near, and so I face the final curtain. My friend, I'll say it clear. I'll state my case, of which I'm certain. I've lived a life that's full. I've traveled each and every highway; and more, much more than this, I did it my way." ("My Way," lyrics by Paul Anka). But Henry hasn't embraced the premise of the lyrics of this song. What a pathetic waste, he thinks, to be so arrogant, haughty, and proud to boast that one has summarily declined the helping hand of the God of Nature; that instead, one's celebration of life has been fueled by an egotistical desire to go it alone! Henry has often wondered how someone could be so ignorant to think that their way is better than the way of Mother Nature. Experience has taught him to walk with Her, to work with Her, and with gratitude to accept Her helping hand whenever it is extended.

"The past, the present, and the future exist as one." (Harriet Beecher Stowe). Henry has felt them breathe together. Time and space, which have no beginning and no end, have defined his final frontiers. They are the bookends to the story of his personally tailored adventures whose design is divine. There is a train bound for glory, and Henry's name is on the passenger manifest. Angels are waiting to check the list twice. During his journey, he is pushing the boundaries of new horizons including the furthest reaches of the wilds above Priest Lake, where he eagerly undertakes new explorations. He is excited to boldly go where no-one has gone before, for he intuitively knows that eternity will be the final stop on that glory train. Henry is determined to follow in the footsteps of Captain James Cook, who declared: "I intend to go not only farther than anyone has been before me, but as far as I think it is possible for anyone to go."

Some believe they have caught a fleeting glimpse of Huckleberry Henry, or perhaps they have just seen the tail of his coonskin cap wagging back and forth, as his shadowy figure retreats into the woods. During colder months, they may have noticed his winter garb of tanned animal hides, hand-sewn with bone awl and sinew. One of the key functions of the fur that has been integrated into his garments is thermoregulation. Before they have been relieved of their coats, furbearers stay cool in hot weather and, more importantly, warm when it's chilly. This is achieved primarily by means of insulation, and one of the best insulators is air. Unlike that of a wolf or a cougar, the fur on Henry's hunting shirt is on the inside, creating a more functional garment with substantial air pockets for warmth, while the leather on the outside more effectively blocks the wind and sheds rain. His lynx mittens tend to be even warmer than his bobcat gloves, and they offer better protection against harsh weather. Unlike the gloves, in the mittens his fingers feel warmer because they are in close contact with each other. Henry has found by sad experience that the gloves he makes are not insulated enough at the tips of the fingers, which are the farthest points from the heart, other than the toes, which can also suffer in the cold. Henry's blood circulation is not as good at his extremities, so they tend to get cold more easily.

Henry's iconic coonskin cap is a symbol of the early American frontier. The style was created by Native Americans who lived in Tennessee and Kentucky. Mountain men from this area took a fancy to the caps and adopted their functional design when they reached the Rocky Mountains. Henry's buckskins are similar to those worn by Native Americans, as well. They have always been popular with frontiersmen and were prized for their warmth and durability. Buckskin jackets were often dyed and elaborately detailed, and were a staple of mountain man clothing. The fringe on Henry's buckskin hunting shirt lets raindrops roll off easily, instead of collecting on the leather. His soft-soled moccasins, stuffed with dried grass or cattail, protect his feet while allowing him to maintain an intimate relationship with the ground. The moccasins of the Plains Indians were hard-soled because their territorial geography prominently featured rock and cacti. The Eastern Indian tribes wore soft-soled moccasins, ideal for walking in leaf-covered forests. Henry has both types, depending upon where his travels might take him. He has adopted the moccasin decorations of the Northern Plains tribes, because their symbols remind him of the beings and places that are sacred to Native American medicine men, and that he hopes will provide him with spiritual protection.

The word moccasin comes from the Powhatan language of eastern Virginian Native Americans. The word stuck because this tribe of the Algonquians was the first to have contact with white settlers. In its broader application, 'moccasin' refers to just about any footwear of indigenous Native Americans. Moccasins are still the most common footwear worn by Henry's Mountain Man peers, and a well-made pair can last for more than 20 years. Their natural leather is very comfortable against bare skin, and those lined with soft, plush fleece provide Henry's feet with an even warmer and cozier feel. He has learned that his soft soled moccasins, even without the perks of cushioned soles, are good for his feet and calf muscles, and obviate the need for supportive features. Moccasins satisfy the therapeutic qualities of minimalist, classic footwear, by adhering to the principle that less is more.

Huckleberry Henry has also adopted the winter clothing and accessories of the Mountain Man. He wears a capote, (pronounced kuh-po-tee), a long coat of simple design, often with a hood. It is made from wool blanket material which can be cut and assembled in the mountains and sewn with a bone awl and sinew. On the rack in his cabin are other assorted fur coats, cloaks, and robes, as well as hats made from beaver fur and raccoon pelts. Although he wears a hat in winter, Henry refutes the myth that a disproportionate amount of body heat is lost through an uncovered head. He insists that wearing a hat simply keeps his head warm, just as wearing any other article of clothing would protect that portion of his covered body. But, he concedes, a hat also keeps his ears warm, which is a nice, comfortable feeling that also reduces the chance of frostbite of those otherwise exposed and vulnerable appendages.

As we read these pages that are adaptations from the *Lost Journal of Huckleberry Henry*, we feel as Helen Keller did. To a world that might have pitied her that she had been dealt a poor hand, she revealed: "It is so pleasant to learn about new things. Every day I find how little I know, but I do not feel discouraged since God has given me an eternity in which to learn more. They took away what should have been my eyes, but I remembered Milton's *Paradise*. They took away what should have been my ears, and Beethoven came and wiped away my tears. They took away what should have been my tongue, but I had talked with God when I was young. He would not let them take away my soul. Possessing that, I still possess the whole." She continued with an expression that Henry would particularly appreciate: "I am conscious of a soul-sense that lifts me above the narrow, cramping circumstances of my life. My physical limitations are forgotten - my world lies upward, the length and breadth and sweep of the heavens (or, as Henry would say, of the Selkirks) are mine!"

Henry's diet has been simple, consisting primarily of whatever he can grow in his garden or forage in the woods, plus fish and wild game. He preserves his meat on drying racks. Over time, he has gathered a variety of knives, including clasp knives, butcher knives, scalpers, bear knives, and skinning knives. Among his prized possessions, however, are his Green River Knife and his Bowie Knife. He carries these on a leather belt, along with a pouch containing his fire-starting kit, a tomahawk, and his "possibles" bag, in which he has stashed everything that could possibly be needed for the day: black powder and measurer, flint and steel, lead balls and patches, a patch knife, and a skinning knife, as well as other personal items. He also carries a ditty bag, that was originally called a "ditto bag" because it contained at least two of everything: needles, spools of thread, buttons, and other similar truck. Perhaps Henry's greatest treasure, however, and his most valuable asset, is his Hawken Rifle. On the early frontier, the Hawken was not mass-produced; rather, each one was painstakingly and lovingly handmade, one at a time. A number of famous mountain men, besides Huckleberry Henry, have owned Hawkens, including Auguste LaCombe, James Beckworth, Hugh Glass, Jim Bridger, Kit Carson, Orrin Porter Rockwell, Joseph Meek, and Jedediah Smith.

When boondocking through the Selkirks, Huckleberry Henry generally manages to eat six indulgent, hearty meals a day to support his regimen of intense physical activity from sunup to sundown. He particularly enjoys the taste of beaver, which has a flavor similar to that of beef or venison, and the bonus is that, before dinner, the beaver provides a hostess gift consisting of a thick, warm pelt. Out on the Crest on a frigid evening in the late fall, a steaming hot beaver stew is exactly what Henry needs to warm his belly and his cheer his spirit. He considers their delicious tails a delicacy.

In his solitude, Henry often recalls the hymns he sang in Church in his youth: "O Lord my God, when I in awesome wonder consider all the worlds Thy Hands have made, I see the stars, I hear the rolling thunder, Thy power throughout the universe displayed." ("How Great Thou Art"). These natural love letters from God continually remind Henry how easily he may find a little bit of heaven to his left and to his right, and before him and behind him. From the exhilarating vantage point of Priest Lake, he senses it most powerfully, however, when he raises his eyes to the Cosmos and views the rich cornucopia of life flowing out in every direction from the nurturing stars.

Huckleberry Henry is not well-read, living in the mountains as he does. He doesn't have a card at the Priest Lake Library, located on Highway 57, just north of the Luby Bay Road cutoff. But he has accumulated a decent collection of books relating to the mountains and from them has gleaned quite a few motivational quotations that reflect his philosophy. Among them, and in no particular order, are the following: Without mountains, we might find ourselves relieved to avoid the pain of the ascent, but we will forever miss the thrill of the summit. ..... It is difficult to live in the mountains, but it is the lowlanders' avoidance of pain that becomes the thief of life. ..... A mountain man's three rules are first, it's always further than it looks. Secondly, it's always taller than it looks. And thirdly, it's always harder than it looks. ..... And finally: Mountains have a way of dealing with overconfidence.

Once or twice a year, Huckleberry Henry meets others of his kind in the valleys beneath the Selkirk Crest. Mountain Man James Beckworth has described the ensuing festivity, as has Henry in his Lost Journal, as a scene of "mirth, songs, dancing, shouting, trading, running, jumping, singing, racing, target-shooting, yarns, and frolic, with all the extravagances that white men or Indians could invent." On quiet evenings at Indian Creek, or at Mosquito Bay, Luby Bay, or Beaver Creek, campers who are tucking their children into their sleeping bags and zipping up their tents can sometimes hear the faint sounds of a genuine Rocky Mountain Rendezvous reverberating off the canyon walls. Though they may be indistinct and are often mistaken for the moaning of the wind in the trees, the howl of a wolf in the distance, or the cry of a cougar up on the Crest, they are as real as the bugle of an elk during the rut, or the excited yips of a pack of coyotes that have gathered around a kill.

Life for Huckleberry Henry hasn't been easy. It's brought him face-to-face with danger and with the threat of death on an uncomfortably regular basis. Sometimes, he has tried to imagine how he will meet his Maker. He wonders if it will follow the drawn-out agony of slow starvation or malnutrition, or if it will be subsequent to the relentless torture of dehydration, burning heat, or freezing cold. Perhaps his jig will be up following the surprise attack of a cougar or wolf, or after being blind-sided by a grizzly bear. Henry often wears a long beard, but not for the sake of vanity. The truth is that it provides him protection from the cold, and it also helps to cushion the blows to his face that are the natural consequence of confrontations in the woods with predators of every size, description, and inclination.

Huckleberry Henry knows that hard work has groomed him for his destiny. He often reminds himself that Abraham Lincoln once said: "I will prepare myself, and someday my chance will come," Henry knows that perspiration must precede inspiration, and that there must be effort before there is excellence. But, better than most, Henry understands that the possession of the world's goods is not wealth, nor is it the real objective of work. "The race is not to the swift, nor the battle to the strong, neither riches to men of wisdom." (Ecclesiastes 9:11). Henry's work ethic orients his moral compass toward righteousness and truth, that the fruits of his labor might be an everlasting dominion, and that without compulsory means, as the dews of heaven, the blessings of the God of Nature might continue to shower down upon him.

In 1812, Huckleberry Henry's forbearers laid the groundwork for the Oregon Trail by locating South Pass, about 35 miles southwest of present-day Lander, Wyoming. This track, that leads through the Rocky Mountains, had eluded Lewis and Clark during their Voyage of Discovery nearly a decade earlier. Just as South Pass was the key to an easier passage by land, so too, the trail system blazed by Henry has created enjoyable routes through the Selkirks from the Lion Creek drainage and Grass Creek into the Pack River drainage and beyond. The Selkirks are between 850 million and 1.5 billion years old, and were thrust by plate tectonics into the sky above a shallow inland sea. Over eons, it had received deposits from the many rivers that emptied into it, and those sediments were lightly metamorphosed. The granite of the Selkirks, however, was formed by complete melting and crystallization of the rock, which makes them igneous by classification. Metamorphic rock, in contrast, is modified only by temperature and pressure, but not by complete melting. Henry probes the present-day drainages of Parker Creek, Pearson Creek, Abandon Creek, Cow Creek, and Smith Creek for routes through the Selkirks, without realizing he is treading on sacred ground whose natural historical record dates back more than a thousand million years.

Winters are long and hard in the high country of North Idaho, and each year Huckleberry Henry anxiously anticipates even the most hopeful signs of spring. Songbirds begin to make their way back home to the Selkirks, and robins and black-capped chickadees are among the first to announce that spring is just around the corner. Their melodious appearance comes well ahead of tulips, daffodils, and the warm breezes that are accompanied by dappled sunshine. Ground squirrels come out in full force, scampering about, and shaking off the stiffness of hibernation. There are subtle changes in light, as well, as the Sun lingers longer in the western sky and days encroach more stubbornly on night. Ladybugs and woolly caterpillars emerge from a long winter spent tucked away in crevices under leaves or bark. Small flying insects are also starting to emerge, but there are no mosquitoes yet. Landmark waterfalls begin their seasonal displays of powerful beauty, and the creeks and streams are full to overflowing. Their cascading water gets more insistently louder as it pounds on river rock and slides furiously over polished granite slabs. Trees begin to awaken and clothe themselves in blankets of tiny buds. April showers come a tad early and the smell of damp earth is in the air. Nature is coming to life as grassy shoots start peeping through the soil and blue skies and sunshine begin to peek through winter's overcast.

Early spring wildflowers compete for Henry's attention, including buttercups, fairy slippers, yellow skunk cabbage, shooting stars, trillium, dogtooth violets, fairybells, nuttal's larkspur, arrowleaf balsamroot, yellowbells, western springbeauty, grass widows, heartleaf arnica, and wild hyacinth. Summer wildflowers shortly follow on their heels, including syringa, death camas, sticky geraniums, prince's pine, honeysuckle, pussytoes, sego lilies, twinflowers, lupine, long-plumed avens, queen's cups, and pink pyrola.

The Summer Solstice is Henry's signal that it is time for Nature to burst forth in its symphonic, orchestral glory. The woodland canopy above his cabin has closed over and the trees are in full leaf, are lovely, and display every shade of green. Spring flowers are fading fast but are quickly being replaced by summer blooms. Henry looks for foxgloves, poppies, and common spotted orchids in the woodlands. In meadows that have come alive with delicate, blue butterflies, bees and hummingbirds are attracted to the sweet-smelling fragrance of honeysuckle, and gather to feed on its nectar. Baby birds make their first tentative fluttering forays beyond the safety of their nests. Many spend a few anxious days on the ground, building their strength and waiting for their feathers to mature before they are ready to take flight. Bats give birth, and by the end of June the pups are independently hunting for insects. Summer evenings in the woods, or near creeks and ponds, are a great time and place for Henry to spot them darting about and swooping through the air, helping to control the revitalized insect population.

Pushing midnight in the middle of summer, Huckleberry Henry has seen "evening make its quiet entrance across the skies, out thru the darkness that, quivering, dies,' while the Milky Way, "beautiful, broad, and white, is fashioned of silver rays and stolen from the ruins of day." Henry watches in wonder as the pale bridge grows, "built by the Architect of night." (Anon). He is also mesmerized by meteor showers including, not only the Aquarids in July and the Perseids in August, but also the Quandrantids in January, the Lyrids in April, the Orionids and Draconids in October, the Taurids and Leonids in November, and the Geminids and Ursids in December.

Some have claimed that deep in the woods, they have stumbled upon Huckleberry Henry's cabin, a mile or two off the well-worn trail that leads from No Telley Basin to Five Mile Ridge. When they have tried to retrace their steps, however, they have been unable to do so. Their topographical maps reveal only that they have been close to his homestead. But when they try to get a compass bearing on his cabin, the needle spins wildly around the dial, as if the Hideaway of Huckleberry Henry does not want to be found.

Others have reported that they've seen smoke rising from what must have been the chimney of his cabin in the woods. But they've been unable to trace it back to its source. Each time they try, a gentle breeze disperses its trail. Some have dismissed the wind-driven smoke as nothing more than morning mist that hangs in the draws above the lake. But others, with a well-developed imagination, have seen in it a pack of wolves, a litter of cougar cubs, or a black bear just coming out of hibernation. The few who listen to the stirrings of the forest have thought they could make out the howl of a wolf, the screech of an owl, or the woof of a nervous grizzly, but they've admitted that it might have been the shout or the cough of a nearby child at play. Just as likely, however, it could have been Huckleberry Henry, mimicking those animals to tease his little Junior Rangers, or test their wilderness acumen.

In autumn, Henry notices that many tree seeds have ripened and fallen to the ground. He looks for plump acorns, shiny brown conkers, and prickly beech mast hidden in the leaf litter at his feet. Damp weather provides ideal conditions for fungi to grow, and autumn is when many species thrive. Mushrooms push their way up through the sphagnum to reveal an amazing range of colors and some very peculiar shapes. Even more weird are the names. From amethyst deceiver to dead man's fingers and lemon disco, to bearded tooth, witch's butter, destroying angel, chicken of the woods, and false turkey tail, these fabulous fungi capture Henry's imagination, and often find their way into his stewpot, to add flavor to a rump roast or venison backstrap.

Henry looks for signs in the fall that betray the possibility of a harsh winter, including the early arrival of the snowy owl (who spends most of its time in the Arctic). Another portentous harbinger of cold weather is the sight of two woodpeckers sharing the same tree. Also heralding the approach of a hard winter season are geese and ducks leaving earlier than usual on their southward migration. Fluffier than normal coats on squirrels, and raccoons with thick tails and bright bands are tell-tale signs that a cold winter is in store. Spiders trying to get into his cabin, and spinning larger-than-normal webs, are for Henry, ominous signs of the early approach of winter. So too is the appearance of ants busily marching to and fro in single file, thicker than normal corn husks, and an abundance of acorns falling from oak trees. Henry also looks for squirrels gathering and storing pine nuts early in the season. The Kootenai, Coeur d'Alene, and Nez Perce Native American tribes had their own long list of signs of early winter, but particularly foreboding for them was the appearance of exceptionally large woodpiles that had been stacked up beside the white-man's cabins that are still found all along Eastshore Road, north of Coolin.

In December 2014, Bonner County absorbed into its maintenance program a 9 mile stretch of Eastshore Road between Indian Creek Bridge and Canoe Point Road. It had previously been privately maintained by a cooperative agreement between the Idaho Department of Lands, the Idaho Department of Parks & Recreation, and the owners of deeded lots in the Huckleberry Bay development. Eastshore Road had been built in the 1950s by loggers, but since then it has provided access to the Lion Head Unit of Priest Lake's campgrounds, as well as to deeded lots and lease cottage sites. Henry is not a huge fan of improvements to the infrastructure around the lake, preferring to leave things in their natural state. He is particularly alarmed that, In the Twenty First Century, campground use has skyrocketed from 9,000 to over 131,000 day users each year. That does not bode well for a reclusive mountain man who prefers to keep his own company and counsel.

To the west of the Selkirk Crest down at lake level, average annual snowfall is 10 feet, but 30-foot depths at higher elevations are not uncommon. Henry has kept meticulous records over the years and has discovered that there are an average of 3 dry days in January, versus 29 in August, which many consider to be the most pleasant month of the year at Priest Lake, weather-wise. There is an average of 73 hours of Sun in February, while there are 330 in August. Precipitation in January averages 6.9 inches, but only 0.8 inches in August. (Typically, 1 inch of rain equals 12 inches of snow). Average humidity in January is 95%. In August, it is 55%. There are 20 average snow days in January. (Henry will let us guess how many there are in August. A dusting is rare, but it can happen up high). There are 15 average fog days in January, but just 1 in August. There is 69% average cloud cover in January, and only 13% during August.

There are roughly 250 billion trees greater than 1" in diameter in America today, which is more than there were a hundred years ago! To Henry's simple mind, it seems that most of them are in the Idaho Panhandle National Forest. (Actually, there are just 1.4 billion trees in the IPNF). Nationally, forest growth has exceeded harvest since the 1940s. In 1997, growth exceeded harvest by 42%, and the volume was 380% greater than it had been in 1920. Land is designated as forest when at least 10% is covered by trees, and the United States is now home to 8% of all the forest area in the world. Idaho has about 21 million acres of forest, 76% of which is owned by the Federal government. 14% of it is in the hands of private landowners, and the state owns about 10%. Idaho's forests are under continual attack from bark beetles, spruce beetles, budworms, tussock moths, western hemlock looper, and other creepy crawlies, as well as from blister rust, root disease and dwarf mistletoe. With so many trees, it is inevitable that some that are diseased will fall on unsuspecting people. Out of necessity, Henry has learned very quickly to identify the tell-tail signs that a tree is in danger of falling, such as dead branches. To fight off invaders, it sheds those branches, generally very unpredictably. Henry also looks for hollow spots in the trunk, caused by decay within the tree. Roots that are raised up and rotten, with mushrooms around the base of the trunk, are warning signs, as well, as are missing leaves close to the trunk. Henry makes it a point to never take a nap in the shade beneath the branches of a diseased tree!

Trees (except for coast redwoods) get their nutrients and water from their roots. When Henry sees leaves falling from the inside, it means that something has compromised the root zone. Big cracks in the trunk, missing bark, or branches that are growing in a tight V-shape, instead of a U-shape, prompt his concern for the tree's health. An unnaturally leaning trunk and exposed roots also get his attention. A lack of topsoil covering the roots exposes them to damage from the elements. Soft spots on the limbs or trunk, due to fungi, are signs of an infestation or an injury. Previous lightning strikes as well as creepy-crawly infestation weaken trees and promote rot. Also, vines can deprive trees of crucial sunlight, contributing to fungal or bacterial disease.

The trees in the IPNF get their nutrients from the soil, but its animals get salt in other, unique ways. Benjamin Franklin White and J.H. Stump began mining salt in 1866, at Stump Creek, which is in southeastern Idaho, near the border with Wyoming. It's about 50 miles north of Soda Springs, known as "the Oregon Trail Oasis" and famous today for its naturally occurring carbonated water geysers. Huckleberry Henry has quickly noticed that his forest friends need salt for survival, but they're not going to get it from a mine, and especially from one so far distant. Instead, herbivores in the Selkirks lick patches of mineral-rich soil and rocks, and in turn, they supply salt to the predators that devour them. Around Priest Lake, animals seek out places where they can lick up salty residues from the ground at sites that are more correctly termed natural mineral licks. A good one can entice grazers from up to 50 miles away. Animals are also attracted to water with dissolved salts like puddles that are drying up, urine, and wet manure. And, by the way, a lot of the insects that buzz around Henry in the summer aren't after his blood. Rather, they just want to lick up his salty sweat.

Around Priest Lake, early prospectors were not looking for salt, but for gold and silver. Unfortunately, they found little, except for up north at the Continental Mine near the Canadian border. In Kalispell Bay, the former Milwaukee Mine site is now a day-use area. Some of the tailings are still visible along the shoreline, and 100 feet offshore are the remains of two sunken wooden boats. (Back in the day, before CraigsList, scuttling was the preferred method of disposing of work boats that had outlived their usefulness.) The Woodrat Mine was in Luby Bay, with a shaft that was 200 feet deep and extended 400 feet eastward, directly under the lakebed. It was worked until the late 1960s.

With Ralph Waldo Emerson, Huckleberry Henry has seen "the spectacle of morning from the hilltop over against his cabin, from daybreak to sunrise, with emotions which an angel might share. The long, slender bars of cloud float like fishes in a sea of crimson light. From the earth, as upon a shore, he looks out into that silent sea. He seems to partake its rapid transformations; the active enchantment reaches his dust, and he dilates and conspires with the morning wind. How does nature deify us with a few and cheap elements!" he has exclaimed. "Give me health and a day," he has declared, "and I will make the pomp of emperors ridiculous."

Even before his disappearance in the woods, Henry had been an avid shed-hunter. Now that he is dependent upon his wilderness survival skills, he has put the sheds he finds to good use. He has fashioned knives, files, whistles, friction fire-sockets, buttons, door handles, candle holders, pot holders, and pressure flakers from the sheds he has come across in the woods. Others, he uses for rustic décor at his cabin. Some, he exchanges for supplies at the Tamrack, leaving the sheds in a pile at a prearranged drop off, and later picking up sugar, salt, gunpowder, lead, and other wilderness necessities, with a few extravagances thrown in for good measure.

Huckleberry Henry utilizes, not only the antlers, but nearly every other element of a harvested big game animal, with the possible exception of the gut-pile. He knows that longer hanging times allow the animal's natural enzymes and acids to break down and tenderize the meat, giving it a smoother, less gamey flavor. He tries his best to keep the meat between 32° and 40° F. He saves the bones for a rich broth that adds zest to his meals. While in the woods, he is always on the lookout for the nests of geese, ducks, and turkeys, and considers it a lucky find when he is able to gather their eggs. Idaho is home to about 11,000 Shiras Moose, up from fewer than 1,000 fifty years ago. That's about half of all moose in the lower 48 states. There are about 107,000 elk in Idaho, as well. Whitetail deer, however, are in decline. The harvest in 2021 was the lowest in 10 years, and 14% lower than 2020, although the highest density is still found in the Panhandle. Henry makes a point to avoid encounters with the 35 to 40 grizzly bears in the Selkirks, preferring to leave them alone to battle it out with the state's 1,500 wolves regarding which of the two species is the apex predator in the region. But Henry is more than happy to concede that title to either of them.

A meteorologist would have taught Huckleberry Henry that in the fall, the jet stream strengthens, and moves south as a river of swiftly moving air in the upper atmosphere. As winter's chill builds in the polar regions, it pushes the jet stream toward the equator. Wind shear climbs markedly, bringing thunderstorms and unsettled weather to the region of the Idaho Panhandle. More often, however, Henry is left to enjoy fall's colors without Nature's accompanying sound and light show. The bright colors of fall foliage that he loves are notably found on the branches of deciduous trees. The word "deciduous" itself stems from the Latin decidere, meaning "to fall off," and the term has come to describe trees that lose their leaves during the autumn as they transition into seasonal dormancy. Deciduous trees have flat, wide leaves that are more susceptible to weather-induced change, when compared to the thin needles of their coniferous cousins. In the Panhandle, Henry notices and appreciates the scattering of deciduous trees among the more prevalent evergreen forests that blanket the region.

Huckleberry Henry has also observed that, in the fall, sunlight decreases, and temperatures drop. What he doesn't realize is that, with those changes, chlorophyll production in broadleaf trees also ramps up, which in turn gives way to the pigments that produce the red, orange, and yellow tones of autumn. At the same time, most of the coniferous trees that surround his cabin (pine, spruce, and firs) maintain their green needles year-round. The exception is the rare subset of larch or tamarack, found in abundance in the Idaho Panhandle, and particularly above No Telley Basin, where their needles turn a brilliant golden color. Therefore, by classification they are deciduous conifers. The needles of all other conifers feature a waxy coating that protects them from the elements, and they produce a natural antifreeze that helps them resist cold weather. Those factors create conditions that allow them to survive the harsh winters along the Selkirk Crest while maintaining their verdant identity.

With the onset of autumn, Henry notices that days grow shorter, and nights get colder. He can see the changes in pigmentation, when carotenoids within the leaves of deciduous trees produce yellow, orange, and brown hues. Anthocyanin pigment contributes a deep red color to turning leaves (as well as to cranberries and apples). The red leaves of autumn are found on the sugar maple, oak, sweetgum, and dogwood that are quite common to New England, while yellow and orange shades are more frequently associated with the hickory, ash, birch, and black maple found in Henry's backyard.

Prior to the terms "fall" and "autumn" making their way into the vernacular, the months of September, October, and November were generally referred to as the harvest season, a time of year for gathering ripened crops. This has become Henry's practical orientation. The use of the word "fall" dates to 1500s England, when the term was a shortened version of "fall of the year" or "fall of the leaf." The 1600s saw the arrival of the word "autumn." By the 18th century, "autumn" had become the predominant name for the season in England, though over the following century, the word "fall" would grow in popularity in the New World. But, while some proper British linguists consider fall to be American slang, the term originated in England, and both "autumn" and "fall" are used interchangeably today. Henry prefers "autumn." The word has a nice ring to it, and more easily 'falls' from his lips.

While Henry attests to the universality of America's reddish and yellow autumnal hues, he is unaware that deciduous trees in Northern Europe are more universally yellow in color. One fascinating theory to explain that phenomenon is that during the ice age of the Pleistocene Epoch, 35 million years ago, the north-to-south orientation of America's mountain ranges allowed for animals on either side to migrate south to warmer climates, whereas the east-to-west orientation of the Alps of Europe trapped many animal species that faced extinction as freezing conditions took hold in the north. The result was that American trees evolved to produce more anthocyanins in their leaves, and thus a darker red color, to help ward off insects, whereas European trees didn't need to do so, since recently extinct insect species no longer posed a threat. This phenomenon has also occurred in East Asia, where forests bear a similar resemblance to those in America, as opposed to the predominantly yellow-hued forests of Northern Europe.

Henry feels very strongly that Nature has invited him to follow along a trajectory that will take him from the launch platform of the clearing in front of his cabin all the way to the farthest reaches of Her creations. His countdown for liftoff has already begun, and has been accentuated by the verb 'to come', as in Come, follow Me." Because Henry has chosen to follow Nature, exactly where, when, and how far he will come only She can determine. This is the way. All Henry can say with any degree of certainty is that his final destination will be out of this world!

Henry understands the value of drinking plenty of water. He is aware that he could become dehydrated through sweating. Like all of us, one of the main ways he loses water is by perspiring. His body is designed to shed excess heat by sweating, which means that he loses more water when his core body temperature rises above its baseline level. Under normal conditions, he loses between 2 and 4 liters of water, per day, through perspiration. In the heat, he can lose 6 or more liters. Henry has found that the best way for him to avoid dehydration in the wilderness is to drink water regularly, avoid strenuous exercise in the heat of the day, try to stay out of the noonday Sun, and wear light clothing for as long as the weather permits.

As Henry traverses the Selkirk Crest, he is never more than a mile or so from reliable water sources. This is because of the generosity of the winter snowpack, and the porous nature of the fractured granite of the mountains and particularly of the ridges above No Telley Basin. He doesn't need to be very creative when exploiting water sources. There will be no wringing mud through a cloth, and no collecting morning dew from the leaves of deciduous trees. The only pathogen he really needs to be aware of is Giardia contamination of rivers, streams, pools, and even springs. As a matter of principle, when he is on the trail, he packs water in with him, or boils it before consumption if it is coming from a local source. On average, Henry needs to drink about 4 liters of water a day to stay adequately hydrated. (Women need about 3 liters a day). The telltale signs of dehydration, in addition to thirst, include dark urine, less frequent urination, dizziness, mood swings and irritability, fatigue, cognitive impairment, headache, muscle cramps, rapid heart rate and breathing, chills, and fever. These diverse symptoms broadly describe the estimated 75% of Americans who remain chronically dehydrated.

Whenever Henry is faced with daunting challenges, he remembers that it is only after he has emerged on the other side of the hourglass of opportunity that he will find expanding horizons and limitless vistas stretching out before him. North Idaho is big sky country, and from the Crest, Henry can see beyond the Selkirks that surround the lake, all the way to the Cabinet Mountains to the east, the Bitterroots to the south, and the Purcells to the north. Their peaks invite him to travel to a far country where eagles make sounds and wolves will abound; where cougars prowl and grizzly bears growl, and the sky is not cloudy all day.

The vegetable garden at Henry's cabin receives light from early in the morning when the Sun peeks over the Crest above Goblin Knob until early evening when it drops behind the notch between Granite and Blacktail mountains. His garden includes lettuce, watermelon, cucumber, and strawberries, which are all good sources of water. In the late fall, winter, and spring, Henry obtains water from snow and ice by melting it in a cauldron set over his campfire. Boiling it ensures the elimination of any dormant pathogens lurking within. He always hydrates before starting out on the day's trek. He knows that his body will only begin to feel "thirsty" when his hydration level is already low. He doesn't play catch-up with hydration. He is always consciously aware of three things: Food, water, and electrolytes, and so while he is bushwhacking in the Selkirks he carries a leather bladder full of water, right next to his ditty bag, his knife, and his possibles bag, and he makes it a point to drink ½ to 1 liter every hour, whether he feels thirsty or not. And then, he drinks even more water after returning to his cabin at the end of the day. He replenishes his electrolytes by eating lots of spinach, kale, broccoli, potatoes, beans, tomatoes, fish, turkey, chicken, and veal.

When reading The Lost Journal of Huckleberry Henry, it immediately becomes obvious that he has been true to the mandate given by Cicero to writers of all ages: "The first law for the historian is that he shall never dare utter an untruth. The second is that he shall suppress nothing that is true. Moreover, there shall be no suspicion of partiality or of malice in his writing." Every page in the narrative of Henry's Journal has been faithful to this mandate.

Huckleberry Henry is a realist and a pragmatist. He understands that as his circle of knowledge expands, so will encroaching borders of darkness. The more he knows, the more he needs to learn. It does no violence to his faith that additional questions to ponder have accompanied his greater understanding of the mysteries of Nature. Fortunately, he has plenty of discretionary time on his hands. His circumstances have blessed him to learn how to budget his time, to give careful attention to the frugality with which he spends his time, and also the diligence with which he makes time, the care with which he finds time, the joy with which he gives time, the wisdom with which he invests time, the pleasure with which he shares time, the frugality with which he buys time, and the discipline he exhibits when taking time. This process allows him to make more time for the accomplishment of things that really matter. Because he has rarely wasted time, seldom bided his time, and hardly ever killed time, he has never yet found that he is out of time.

Henry is not a religious man in the organizational or denominational sense; nevertheless, he intuitively understands that faith, light, and truth are common irreducible denominators that have established the baseline upon which he has acquired practical knowledge. As a pragmatist, he is never one to turn his back on Divine Providence. He won't look a gift horse in the mouth. As a child, he remembered his mother reading to him from Alice's Adventures in Wonderland. Alice asked the Cheshire Cat: "Would you please tell me which way I ought to go from here?" The cat responded: "That depends a good deal on where you want to go." "I admit," responded Alice, "I don't much care where." Said the cat: "Then it doesn't matter which way you go." "Just so I go somewhere!" implored Alice. "Oh," responded the cat, "you are sure to do that, if you walk far enough." Henry does not engage in aimless walkabouts in the Selkirks. Whenever he sets out from his cabin, he has already formulated in his mind a plan for the day, but he is flexible enough in his thinking to make room for Nature to caper. Had he been a seafaring man, he might have said: "let's see what the tide brings in!"

Henry is a sight to behold. He is as a child coming down like gentle rain through darkened skies with glory trailing from his feet as he goes, and with endless promise in his eyes. He is a stranger from a realm of light, who has forgotten all - the memory of his former life and the purpose of his call. He is never truly alone in the Selkirks, as long as he comprehends the whispering wind when he looks up at the stars at night, revealing who he really is and why he is here. Huckleberry Henry is a warrior saved to fight the battles raging in the hearts of men on the last day of the world.

It is apparent that as Henry has recorded his impressions in his Journal, his experiences have become a springboard for personal enlightenment. He may not recognize it, but as he has come to terms with the Selkirks, he has probed the mind of God, which is, after all, the final frontier of exploration. He has been introduced to the wonders of exciting new dimensions of experience, blessing him with refreshing ways of looking at life, and in doing so has caught a glimpse of eternity. As he looks up at the heavens from No Telley Basin, it is easy for him to visualize himself living among the stars, traveling to a far country where few have gone before. Through the ministrations of Nature, he better understands the abode of the Gods.

During their first encounter, Bearclaw Chris Lapp had told Jeremiah Johnson something that would have resonated with Huckleberry Henry: "I know who you are, declared Bearclaw. "You're the same dumb pilgrim I've been hearing for twenty days and smelling for three." Jeremiah, like Henry, had not yet developed the savoir faire necessary to survive in the wilderness, but he knew enough to know he didn't know much. He asked his mentor: "If I head due west tomorrow, will I find good places to trap?" Bearclaw immediately responded: "If you head due west or any other direction tomorrow, you'll be a starvin' pilgrim in a week. You ain't likely to meet up with someone of my good nature. The mountain's got its own ways." Henry, who has spent time in the Selkirks, knows what he meant by that simple statement.

Jeremiah Johnson had several encounters with Bearclaw, "blood kin to the grizzer that bit Jim Bridger's ass." They are reminiscent of the exchanges Huckleberry Henry has had with various Selkirk "brush-apes" over the years, those whom he met who found themselves in similar circumstances in the high country along the Crest. On one occasion, Jeremiah had a chance encounter with Bearclaw, after several months of solitude. He asked: "Would you happen to know what month of the year it is? No," Bearclaw responded, "I truly wouldn't. I'm sorry pilgrim. March, maybe. I don't believe April." He continued, "Winter's a long time going, huh? Stays long this high." And then, he gently added: "You've done well to keep so much hair when so many's after it, Jeremiah. I hope you will fare well."

Avalanches are common in the mountains surrounding Priest Lake, and they can take even the most experienced outdoorsmen by surprise. As Bear Claw revealed to Jeremiah: "Avalanche took the cabin. Lost my mule. We swum out of it. But no matter. Weren't no griz left anyway." Red flags that Henry looks for when traveling in avalanche country include signs of recent slides and of unstable snow, such as cracking or collapsing snowpack, and whumping and hollow drum-like sounds on hard snow. Avalanche danger increases after heavy snowfall or rain, if high winds have loaded snow on leeward slopes, and if the weather suddenly becomes significantly warmer. He is wary of steep, smooth, leeward slopes. Windward slopes that have been stripped by wind are usually safer than leeward slopes that have been loaded. Within the snowpack, Henry will often dig a pit for proper identification of dangerously weak layers. He has found that avalanches are possible on any slope steeper than 30 degrees and that they occur most frequently on slopes between 35 and 50 degrees.

Avalanches may be triggered along ridge crests, or from flatter areas in the runout zone. Henry studies cornices that reveal prevailing wind direction and for signs that the slope below is wind-loaded. He knows that slopes with gullies, steep-sided creek bottoms, or slopes that end in depressions can be deadly terrain traps because of the high probability of a deep burial should he be caught in a slide. He knows if he is buried, he is not getting out alive. If he must put himself in harm's way, he favors slopes that are fan-shaped at the bottom and do not have obstacles like rocks or trees to crash into. Concave bowls are nasty traps because fractures propagate around the slope and all the debris collects at the bottom, but slopes with natural anchors like trees and boulders can provide some protection from slides.

At another chance encounter up high, Bearclaw walked into Jeremiah's camp, and asked: "What's on the spit?" "Grown particular?" responded Jeremiah. "Not about feedin'. Just the company I keep. You've come far, pilgrim," observed Bearclaw, as he accepted a bit of meat. "Feels like far," said Jeremiah. "T'were it worth the trouble?" "Ha? What trouble." As he got up to leave, Bearclaw told Jeremiah: "You cook good rabbit, pilgrim." As Del Gue exclaimed on another occasion as he parted ways with Jeremiah, with Gue headed for the Musselshell, so could it be said of Huckleberry Henry, who remained comfortably situated high above Five Mile Ridge and snugly tucked well back into No Telley Basin: "Ain't what we got here somethin'? I told my mam and pap I were goin' to be a mountain man, and they acted like they'd been gut-shot. 'Make your life here,' they said. 'Here's where the peoples is. Them mountains is for Indians and wild men.' Mother Gue, said I, the Selkirks is the marrow of the world, and by God, I was right! Here, I can keep my nose in the wind and my eyes along the skyline."

Who can say how Huckleberry Henry came across most of the "truck" that he has accumulated over the years as he has scratched out a living in the mountains? Perhaps, from time to time, he just got "lucky" and would stumble upon a particularly generous "find", as had Jeremiah Johnson, who encountered the frozen corpse of Hatchet Jack in the winter wilderness. Clutched in Jack's hands was his rifle, with a note attached: "I, Hatchet Jack, bein' of sound mind and broke legs do hereby leaveth my bear rifle to whatever finds it. Lord hope it be a white man. It is a good rifle and kilt the bear that kilt me. Anyway, I am dead. Yours truly, Hatchet Jack." Later, Del Gue told Jeremiah (the new owner of the 50 caliber Hawkin): "That Hatchet Jack was a wild one. Lived with a she mountain lion in a cave up on the Musselshell. She never did get used to him."

Del echoed a sentiment that would become increasingly familiar to Huckleberry Henry, exclaiming: "By God, I are a mountain man, and I'll live until an arrow or a bullet finds me, and then I'll leave my bones right here on this great map of the magnificent!" Priest Lake country would have resonated with Del Gue, as it has with Henry. It is the Crown Jewel of North Idaho and from its many facets are reflected year-round access to some of the most diverse and incredible terrain, scenery, and outdoor recreation that Idaho has to offer. It is not a tableau for the timid; rather it is, as Del exclaimed, a great map of the magnificent, reserved for those with the hearts, souls, and sinews of mountain men and women.

Each morning, when Huckleberry Henry shakes off the cobwebs from his mind, he says to himself: "This is a new day that God has given me to spend as I will. In exchange for 24 hours of my life, I can waste it or use it for good. But of one thing I am certain. When tomorrow comes, today will be gone forever, leaving something in its place that I have traded for it. I want it to be gain, not loss, good, not evil, and success, not failure. I want it to be worth the price I've paid for it." Henry is determined to use what talents he may possess, knowing that the woods would be very quiet if no birds sang except those that sang best. His ideals are like stars. He can't touch them with his hands. But like a seafarer, he chooses them as his guides, and following them, he is certain that he will reach the landfall of his destiny.

With the poet, Huckleberry Henry has mused: "I wish I could remember the days before my birth, and if I knew the God of Nature before I came to earth. In quiet moments when I'm all alone, I close my eyes and envision my mountain home. Although I can't remember and cannot clearly see, I listen to the spirit and so I must believe. But still I wonder, and I hope to find the answer to the question that is on my mind. Is No Telley Basin the prototype of heaven? Is it very far? I would like to know if it's beyond the brightest star." (Adapted from Janice Kapp Perry, "Where is Heaven?"). Henry would probably say that his working definition of heaven is all around him, manifest   as his mountain home beside the still waters of the Crown Jewel of North Idaho.

When he will be away from his cabin overnight, Huckleberry Henry is meticulous about finding a good spot to set up camp early in the day. He knows that location is the most important thing to consider when choosing a site. He avoids those that are exposed, or near lone trees, high ridges and mountain tops, and other likely lightning targets. Instead, he looks for spots with boulders or other natural contours that provide protection from the wind. but he stays clear of unhealthy trees while making the most of Sun and shade. He prefers smooth level ground with good drainage near a water source, but away from valleys, canyons, and banks of small, shallow rivers that are susceptible to flooding. If he is pitching a tent, he orients its door toward the rising Sun in the east. He maintains an organized and clean camp, keeps his trash at a distance, and his stash in a bear bag that has been slung at least 10 feet off the ground, over the branch of a tree at least 100 feet away from his bedroll.

Huckleberry Henry considers at least five factors of wilderness survival to stay safe and comfortable in his camp. These include wind, water, widowmakers, wood, and wildlife. Henry's body expends energy to keep his core temperature warm, so when it is cold and windy, he takes special precautions to cover himself so that he will not be needlessly robbed of heat. He also orients his shelter to block the prevailing wind. He has witnessed the hazards associated with running or standing water in stormy weather, so he tries to pick a campsite on elevated ground away from drainage pathways, but still near a reliable water source. He is aware of widowmaker trees and branches that could be fatal hazards should they fall, even if there is little or no wind. He knows that having adequate fuel for his fire will help him to pass the night more comfortably and could ultimately spell the difference between life and death. This means gathering enough has to offer, kindling, and logs to see him through until morning, using whatever the landscape has to offer. He looks for animal tracks, scat, and game trails to gauge wildlife activity in the area, and he takes necessary precautions to protect himself and his camp from opportunistic predators. Watching his top-knot means paying attention to every detail, so that he can get the rest during the night that he needs and deserves.

The four basic needs in nearly all survival situations are shelter, water, food, and fire. In the harsh environment of the Idaho Panhandle North of The Narrows at Priest Lake, Henry could survive for upwards of 3 minutes without oxygen, and for around 30 minutes in icy water. He would last for 3 hours without shelter in the bitter cold of winter, for 3 days without water and for 3 Weeks without food in the balmy days of summer. But sooner or later, even if he had air, shelter, water, and food, he would sooner or later need fire to supplement the heat that the engine inside his body supplies to keep his core temperature at a constant 37° C. He needs to stay warm if he wants to think clearly and make good decisions, a lesson he learned the hard way in the days following his disappearance below the Wigwams in late October.

Those who boondock in the backcountry are advised to watch their own top-knots as they keep an eye out for Henry and listen for signs of his presence. But they are unlikely to hear his voice. Over the years, he has learned to keep his own counsel, and to carefully choose his words. As Jeremiah Johnson once observed: "It's been a long time since I had so much of the English language spoke at me. I ain't used to it. Nothin' wrong with quiet. It's a lot easier than sayin' all that gibberish."

Huckleberry Henry has now lived for years in isolation in the wilderness above Priest Lake, but he is still a ticketed passenger on Spaceship Earth, which is a modest and unassuming vessel negotiating a vast cosmic ocean. The cost of his voucher is like any other, but it won't be redeemed until he has reached eternity. His Captain only asks Henry to follow His charted Plan and to trust in His provident navigational skills. During Henry's journey, his Creator's enlightened approach to education gives him the opportunity to learn from his mistakes, and to make his own individual course corrections without suffering from irreparable consequences that could be eternally damaging.

Huckleberry Henry doesn't have the metaphysical skills to divine the future by simply plotting the position of the stars that wheel with celestial precision across the night sky. (Of course, he knows that it is the earth rotating on its axis, rather than heaven, that moves.) But still, he has been able to chart the coordinates that mark his eternal progress as he witnesses the ethereal light that dances about the glittering jewels that have been deposited by God to define the boundaries of the Cosmos.

As Henry looks up in wonder at the night sky, he wonders how many stars he can see with just his naked eye. The total, as it turns out, comes to a paltry 9,000 that are visible across the entire sky in both hemispheres. If he were thinking as a scientist, he would realize that he can see about 1 star per cubic parsec (one second of arc). But if he were at the core of our galaxy, Henry could see 100 times that many, and if he were inside one of the Milky Way's many globular clusters, he could see 1,000 stars per cubic parsec. Both the day and the night sky would be filled with over 4.5 million visible stars! Their light would be so bright that it would permeate all of space and fill the entire sky, so that Henry might think that he was nigh unto the throne of God, instead of the Selkirk Crest.

We can imagine that, in the first few days following his disappearance, Huckleberry Henry quickly learned how to set up a wilderness camp. The first step in his preparation would have been to build a fire bed. A strong foundation for his campfire would be crucial for both a good fire and for safety. He would have first cleared a small area and set large rocks around the fire bed for insulation. He would have cleared the area of any flammable materials, such as bushes, plants, fallen branches, dead grass, and leaves. Then, the preparation of the bed itself would have begun.

Henry would intuitively know that to start a fire, three essential conditions would need to be met. He would need to find a way to achieve the ignition temperature of a combustible material in the presence of oxygen. He would need to gather and segregate three types of flammable material: tinder to get it started, kindling to help it to grow, and firewood to keep it going. Tinder includes small twigs, dry leaves, and needles or forest duff. Kindling consists of small sticks. Firewood is composed of larger pieces of wood to keep the fire going through dinner, into the evening, and throughout the darkest and coldest hours of the night. Henry would find wood by foraging for dead, fallen branches. After many years perfecting his technique, his best fires still rely on dry wood. The drier it is, the easier it has been for him to get the fire started and the less smoke there will be. He checks the wood by breaking it in half. Dry wood always breaks easily and feels brittle to the touch, but if it bends, it is wet.

When making a campfire in the evening, Henry has several designs from which to choose. First, he can make a Tepee or Cone fire. One of the classic fire shapes, it gets its name from the shelter it resembles. Henry finds it to be particularly useful when his firewood is a bit damp. To build it, he puts a small amount of tinder in the center of the pit. Then, he stacks kindling around the tinder in the shape of a tepee, adding larger logs around it in a similar tepee shape. His tepee fires produce lots of heat and burn fast. They have a circular base with a wide diameter that lets in lots of air. They are typically built for warmth, but can be useful for cooking, as well. The strong flames are good for preparing food that has been suspended in a cooking pot below a tripod. Tepee fires also burn down well, leaving nice beds of coals upon which cast iron skillets may be positioned with stability.

Its wide, flat design makes a Log Cabin fire easy to build and to light, and creates a nice hot bed of coals which are perfect for the preparation of a campfire meal. In fact, Henry often has a hard time deciding which fire design is better, the tepee or the Log Cabin style. To build a log cabin fire, he puts plenty of tinder in the center, in the shape of a small tepee. Then, he places two pieces of firewood logs parallel to each other with a big gap in the middle, then another two pieces on top, at right angles, adding additional levels as needed. After he lights the tinder, he maintains the fire by feeding wood through the sides of the cabin. Even if the larger logs are damp, they will dry out as the fire burns.

Occasionally, Henry chooses to build a Platform or Upside-Down Pyramid fire. Because it is started on top of the wood, the fire burns down into the logs instead of up and out of them. This creates a solid, flat platform of hot coals that are perfect for cooking, since a pot can be set directly on the coals, and the fire will sustain itself as it burns.

He might choose a Star Fire, or Indian Fire, that is often depicted as the campfire of the old West. Six or so logs are laid out like the spokes of a wheel, in a star shape. The fire is started at the "hub," and each of the logs is pushed towards the center as the flames consume the inner ends. Henry often chooses this design when he is settling down for the evening, keeping a stick nearby to push the logs in closer to the center during the night.

When it looks like he could be caught out in the weather, Henry sometimes chooses to build a Lean-to fire, which creates a protective canopy under which a tinder bundle can be placed. This design works well on windy or rainy days with the firewood acting as a shield to help get the first flames going. The trade-off is that airflow is restricted, so it can be a bit harder to get the fire going. This is one reason why Henry always keeps his tinder dry. To build his Lean-to campfires, he lays a long piece of wood within the fire ring, and then leans smaller pieces of kindling against the top side of the longer piece. Then, he puts tinder beneath this, lighting the fire and continuing to add tinder and kindling to keep it burning until it is self-sustaining.

With all these fires, Henry first lights the tinder, and once the flames catch, he blows very gently to feed the fire with oxygen and then continues to build the fire using additional kindling. Once he has a small fire going, he starts adding larger pieces of wood, resisting the temptation to add too many logs too early, which could smother the fire and extinguish any flame. Henry finds it difficult to remove wood once he has added it, so he errs on the side of caution, adding more fuel only if the fire isn't initially big enough.

He always waits for a bed of glowing coals to form in the pit before cooking his dinner or roasting s'mores. This can take up to 45 minutes. Sometimes, he divides his fire in half, raking the glowing coals to one side, and allowing the other side to burn with an open flame. That gives him different levels of heat upon which to cook, making the fire more versatile. Henry is always careful when extinguishing his fire, leaving it attended until it is cold-out. He knows that any residual heat could easily reignite partially burned logs and cause a forest fire.

In the winter, when he is miles from the split, dried, and stacked wood tucked under the eaves of his cabin, things are more challenging for Huckleberry Henry. When it is time to start a fire, he needs to cover a lot of ground to find the required items. He is always careful to remain aware of his surroundings and familiar landmarks as he tramps through the woods, because this is the time when many tenderfoot campers get disoriented and become lost. As he walks, he is mindful of items that could be useful for starting a fire, and he always carries his ditty bag on his belt, with items he might need.

It is small, dry, and brittle fire-starter materials that he is looking for. When the ground is covered by snow, he looks for dead trees with exposed limbs that he can easily break off. He keeps an eye out for dry moss, for lichens, and for witches' hair that has caught on the rough bark of Douglas fir. As he moves up to larger material, he looks for dry wood under fallen trees, within tree wells, or inside their drip line.

Henry's first order of business is gathering kindling, working up from matchstick to pencil thickness size, and then to finger and thumb sized fragments of wood. He uses his knife and hatchet to shave material from larger pieces. After gathering an armload, he turns his attention to proper fuel, starting with sticks about half the width of his wrist and moving on to logs about the size of his forearm.

Lastly, for maintaining his campfire, Henry looks for log size pieces. For every hour of fire he wants, he needs to gather two armloads of material. To tend a small fire all night, he needs a stack that is pretty much waist-high! Obviously, the larger the fire, or the colder the anticipated night, the more fuel he will need. Long winter nights require a lot more fuel than short, balmy summer evenings.

To light his fire when there is snow on the ground, Henry looks for an area out of the elements, dry if possible, or under some tree limbs (if the branches aren't heavily laden with snow). If the snow isn't too deep, he digs his fire pit down to dirt. But if he is only making a fire to cook a meal or to boil water, he just stomps down on the snow to make a stable, level platform. If he intends to maintain the fire overnight, he digs down through the snow to find solid ground. In any case, over time, the fire will melt the snow all the way to dirt.

The same as with a regular fire, Henry makes a 'nest' or a cave with the materials he's collected, starting with tinder and kindling, keeping the larger material off until his fire is burning nicely. Airflow is essential. Blowing on his fire stokes the embers, and once the smaller material is burning well, he keeps adding larger fuel until his campfire is self-sustaining.

If he is going to establish a wilderness camp for some time, and particularly when the ground is snow-free, Henry takes the time to line his fire pit with granite, marble, or slate, which is dense and much less likely to have absorbed water and unexpectedly explode when exposed to prolonged heat. He is always on the lookout for soapstone, because it is a metamorphic rock consisting of talc with other minerals that has the capacity to hold heat well. In the bottom of the pit, he first spreads a layer of sand and then gravel, if he can find these materials, to provide a good base layer beneath the coals.

Huckleberry Henry's Lost Journal has surrendered a few more motivational quotes: In concert with Earth and sky, woods and fields, and lakes and rivers, mountains are excellent schoolmasters, and teach us more that we could learn from books. ..... Keep putting one foot in front of the other, and one day you will look back and see that you've climbed a mountain. ..... Sleeping bags are the soft tacos of the bear world. ..... Be like a mountain; touch the sky but stay rooted to the ground. ..... When preparing to climb a mountain, pack a light heart. ..... It is a crude meal, but the best of all entrés is hunger, when you are alone in the mountains. ..... There may be no WiFi in the mountains, but it is there that you will find a better connection. ...... There is no better time to recharge your spiritual batteries than when you find yourself in the embrace of Mother Nature while in the mountains.

When January rolls around, Huckleberry Henry worries that long winter blues may lie ahead. Sometimes, it seems that the God of Nature no longer speak to him. During trials of his faith, he has wondered if the Creator of the Idaho Panhandle National Forest can speak at all. Perhaps He has suffered a massive stroke resulting in aphasia. Maybe He has lost His First Amendment rights, and no longer enjoys freedom of speech. Maybe He has developed xenophobia and has retreated behind the granite walls of Lion Creek in response to the strident voices of those who insist that He does not exist. Maybe He just doesn't care about Henry anymore. His silence might be evidence that He has lost interest in His mountain man, has other things on His mind, has other priorities or other projects to occupy His attention, or perhaps He has become distracted by more pressing, concerns. Maybe He has finally realized that Henry just doesn't need Him anymore. Maybe Henry is doing well enough on his own in the wilderness.

Maybe the God of Nature is sitting back and taking a much-needed respite from His responsibilities because technology has taken His place, science has satisfied all of Henry's needs, and rationalization has assuaged his conscience. Maybe He is daunted by Twenty-first Century advances in the healing arts and feels that His therapeutic powers have become obsolete. Maybe the explosion in information technology has intimidated Him. Maybe He feels overshadowed by our society's advances in education, that conventional wisdom has replaced divine direction, and that there is no longer a need for pointed, specific, and individual heavenly instruction.

Maybe the God of Nature has grown tired of competing against the avalanche of negative press that spews forth from a media that has its own agenda. Maybe He has been overawed by the mesmerizing wonders of C.G.I. and social media and feels that His miracles cannot possibly compete with the enchantments of Industrial Light and Magic. Maybe He has nothing to add to the dialogue, because Henry and others like him have figured things out on their own and are securely in control of their own destiny. But, maybe, none of the above is true, which begs the questions for Henry: Are there long winter blues ahead, or are they just the physical manifestations of the icy breath of evil. Henry's positive, motivational, and inspirational Journal entries point to the latter, and reflect his refusal to surrender his free will and his destiny to the capricious whims of the Adversary. Instead, he warms himself before the fire of his faith.

When selecting a winter campsite, Henry always looks for a spot that has protection from the wind and isn't susceptible to avalanches, hazardous trees, or branches that might fall in the middle of an otherwise peaceful night. He always identifies landmarks near his campsite to make it easier to find his way back to shelter in case he is caught in a storm while exploring the nearby woods. He avoids camping in spots that are shady in the morning. Before setting up his tent, he packs down the snow so it will not easily melt beneath his bedroll during the night. Digging a lower vestibule provides more storage area, conserves heat, and makes it easier to get in and out of his tent.

It is very important for Henry to consciously consume plenty of calories when he is camping in winter, as digestion helps generate heat. When winter boondocking, his goal is to consume up to 10,000 calories a day, and he also makes sure to stay hydrated. He stores his water bottle upside down, since in very cold weather it will freezes from the top down. But he never eats snow rather than melting it, because he'd waste calories converting the solid to liquid. Instead, he lets his campfire do the work!

When he is camping on top of deep snow and needs to answer the call of nature, if he finds himself without toilet paper, he uses snow in a pinch. During the other seasons of the year, there are generally lovely soft dombeya leaves nearby (aptly named "the toilet paper plant"). Common mullein, broadleaf plantain, curly dock, lamb's ear, and cottonwood, are also great substitutes that are sustainable sources of 'toilet paper'. There are other uses for these big-leafed plants, too. Henry uses them as face wipes and wound bandages. But he hadn't been in the woods for long before he learned, by sad experience, to never wipe his rear with a leaf unless he was certain of its identity (the leaf, not his bum)! And, by the way, Henry doesn't hold in his pee, either, knowing his bladder would needlessly expend energy just to keep his urine warm.

Henry has lots of choices when deciding which type of wilderness oven or stove to build. Some of his best options include stone stoves, including trench, pit, mound, and hillside configurations. He knows that building a stone stove or an outdoor survival oven is almost always a better option than maintaining an open fire, with a kettle. His internally fired ovens are usually made of very large stones that radiate heat for some time. Ovens are initially heated by simply building up the fire for a couple of hours. Henry has found that just about any tight pile of suitable rocks with a hole in the middle and a door in the front will satisfy the requirements of an oven.

To make a typical square oven, Henry constructs three walls out of stone, places one or more large, wide rocks on top to form the roof, and caulks all the gaps with clay, that can often be found on the banks of nearby creeks or along dry riverbeds. This helps his fire to burn hotter, as the only entry for air will be the draught hole (the doorway at the base of the stove), which is also where he feeds sticks into the fire once it is going. Henry places draught holes on the sides of his stone stove, using just one at a time while closing off the other, depending upon the direction of the prevailing wind.

Lastly, Henry looks for a stone that will snugly fit in the front of the oven to serve as a door. An opening on the top at the back serves as a chimney. Once built, Henry fires the oven right away, leaving the door ajar to allow it to breathe. It might take some time, but once it is going, it will radiate heat for hours, for both cooking and comfort.

These stone stoves or ovens are much better options for cooking than open fires. The heat is contained in the enclosure and most of it is concentrated in the center, beneath Henry's pot, right where he wants it. He hangs the pot on a center pole, so that it just touches the top of the stove, to better absorb the heat. He also has the option to use a pan on top of the stove for cooking or for smoking meat or fish.

Henry's trademark stone stoves are either round or square, and observant hikers in the Selkirks sometimes come across them at his abandoned camps, although they are generally off the beaten track. Sometimes, the center pole (or ridge pole) of his stoves is still intact, supported on each end by a tripod. They look for remnants of his campfire or stove in the shade of tree branches, being familiar with his habit of positioning the stove so that if it were to rain, he could more easily rig a canopy overhead. When hikers have come across an abandoned campsite, they find it quite satisfying to set up their own tents in the same location, rebuild his stoves that have been at the mercy of the elements, kindle a fire, cook a meal, and go to sleep after telling each other stories of Henry's exploits.

When Henry hasn't had the time, resources, or need to build a stone stove, he has often quickly built a cooking fire by digging a trench with square sides, 18 inches wide, a foot deep, and a couple of feet long. Because such a fire is made in a hole, the wind isn't as much of an issue as it would be, were he to have built a normal campfire above ground. To go first-class, he sometimes walls up the sides of the trench with rocks, to create radiant heating. When he hangs his kettle on a center pole, in no time he'll have a steaming cup of hot cocoa cradled in his hands to warm both his spirit and his belly.

By creating a hot rock heating pit in the dirt floor of his shelter, Henry can enjoy the heat of a fire with little danger to himself or the shelter (see below). He starts by digging a small pit a little bigger than the bowling ball sized rock that he will be using to transfer heat. He sculpts the hole to match the rock's size and shape, finding another one that is flat and dry, and that won't explode when heated, to cover the pit. Sometimes, he recesses the rock lid so that it will sit flush with the dirt floor. Finally, he heats up his pit stone in a separate fire for about an hour, carries the stone to the pit with a shovel, drops it in, and seals it with the flat stone lid. Then, all that remains is for Henry to bask in luxuriant radiant heat that will last for several hours. He has recorded a word of caution in his Lost Journal: Don't set fire to your blankets as Jeremiah Johnson did after making a hot rock heating pit, or hot coal bed, to sleep on. As Jeremiah was swatting out the flames that had ignited his bedding in the middle of the night, Bearclaw Chris Lapp, who had been sleeping nearby, dryly remarked, before turning over and closing his eyes again: "Didn't put enough dirt down. Saw it right off."

For sustained heat, Henry always has at the ready another rock of a similar shape and size to the first rock so that when it has cooled off, the second rock can be swapped out to maintain the heat. This trick works best in dry soil with red hot rocks.

Tramping through the snow beneath a starry sky is always a remarkable experience for Huckleberry Henry. In winter at Priest Lake, and without light pollution, the stars appear brighter and clearer, and seem to pop out at Henry. This is because, at this point during its year-long journey around the Sun, the Earth is facing out towards the edge of the Milky Way galaxy, rather than inward toward its star-dense center which gives the night sky a hazy quality. As an additional bonus, there are no mosquitoes or ticks, fewer humans in the woods, and pesky bears that could become a nuisance at other times of the year have drifted off into the dreamless sleep of hibernation.

Henry is lucky to have a down sleeping bag that is twice as warm as synthetic materials of the same weight. He always wears a base layer of clothing to wick away moisture, a middle layer to retain body heat, and an outer layer to protect against the wet and the wind. A hat, balaclava, gloves, sunscreen, goggles, Darn Tough socks, and boots round out his winter wardrobe accouterments.

Countless times, on moonless nights, long after families who are vacationing at the lake have finished making s'mores and have retreated from their firepits, and the children have been tucked into bed, Henry has lingered nearby in the darkness, to dream with the mystics who see "torrents of light and rivers of the air, along whose bed the glimmering stars are as gold and silver sands in some ravine, where mountain streams have left their channels bare." He witnesses the God of Nature "descend in the sheen of celestial armor, on serene and quiet nights, when all the heavens are fair," and he marvels at the stardust that has "whirled aloft and flown from His invisible chariot wheels." (William Wordsworth, "The Galaxy").

As fate would have it, Henry has lived a solitary life, and has accepted his lot without complaint. Still, as he retreats from the firepit and heads back to No Telly Basin, he prays that he will not end up as 'the man, with soul so dead, who never to himself hath said, 'This is my own, my native land!' Whose heart hath ne'er within him burned, as home his footsteps he hath turned from wandering on a foreign strand! If such there breathe, go, mark him well; for him no Minstrel raptures swell. High though his titles, proud his name, boundless his wealth as wish can claim; despite those titles, power, and pelf, the wretch, concentered all in self, living, shall forfeit fair renown, and, doubly dying, shall go down to the vile dust from whence he sprung, unwept, unhonoured, and unsung." (Longfellow, "The Lay of the Last Minstrel").

Henry has many options from which to choose when building wilderness shelters, including snow caves, tarp wings, and burritos, A-frames, and bough beds. His choice is dictated by many factors, including weather conditions, local topography, available materials, presence or absence of predators, and length of stay. Protection from the harsh elements is the principle that guides his efforts.

Even as he makes his campfire, Henry is already planning the design of his wilderness shelter, which is a top priority that when properly constructed, decreases the likelihood of a survival emergency. Exposure to the unforgiving elements in severe weather conditions can be deadly within a few hours without some type of shelter as a first line of defense. Luckily, there is an array of techniques and materials that Henry utilizes to neutralize pending emergencies. The Round Lodge is one of them. It is a hybrid from many cultures. Part tepee, part wicki-up, and influenced by many architectural styles, a Round Lodge blocks wind, rain, cold, and Sun. It is structured like a tepee, with the addition of a solid doorway, and typically has a smoke hole through the roof to accommodate a small fire for heat and light. Henry often thatches this shelter with grass or mats; or he coats it with a thick layer of leaf litter. Lodge styles like this abounded in the American West. It has worked equally well in wetter climates, and there is evidence that it was even used millennia ago in pre-Roman Britain.

From the dust, Ralph Waldo Emerson may as well as have been speaking to Huckleberry Henry and to those of us who share his passion for the outdoors, when he counseled: "Hitch your wagon to a star." Emerson knew that when we bind our fortunes to the heavens, we break free from normal temporal constraints. The jewels that Nature has scattered on the beaches of our lives are of every color and hue, created when they have been subjected to temperature or pressure. Conversely, when we're gliding effortlessly through life, we can be pretty sure that we're going downhill. It seems that, if we want to make real progress, we will likely encounter healthy doses of opposition along an uphill journey that is full of potholes, washouts, kelly humps, and other obstacles. So, hitching our wagons to the heavens is sound advice.

In wilderness survival situations, without the mental discipline to stay focused on the tasks at hand, Huckleberry Henry would have found himself distracted by telestial targets and would have been unable to see the forest for the trees. For example, he might have looked to the Milky Way to catalogue its stars and constellations while at the same time neglecting to recognize his more accessible and tangible blessings. If Henry had fallen victim to such a myopic view, he would have been hampered by a rev-limiter on the power plant that fuels not only his thoughts and actions, but also the galaxies in the heavens. He might have been drawn to the light, but only as moths are to fire, and he would have done so without purpose or direction. He would have aimlessly fluttered about without making substantive changes. Higher level thinking would have forever remained just beyond the reach of his comprehension. Fortunately, living in the woods has endowed Henry with humility, and he rarely falls into the trap of blind self-sufficiency. Sometimes, despite the abundance of venison, elk jerky, quail eggs, and dandelion salad, Henry's only menu items have left him choosing between humble pie and eating crow. But this fare has nourished his constitution and has only made him stronger in challenging situations.

From the front stoop of his cabin in No Telley Basin, Henry looks up at the same stars as did Hawkeye, adopted son of Chingachgook, the last of the Mohicans. He remembers how Hawkeye had told Cora Munro: "At the birth of the Sun and of his brother the Moon, their mother died. So, the Sun gave to the Earth her body, from which was to spring all life. And he drew forth from her breast the stars, and these he threw into the night sky to remind him of her soul." (James Fenimore Cooper). As Henry's finger traces their patterns in the air, he remembers how Cora had said of her experience: "It was more deeply stirring to my blood than any imagining could possibly have been." That is a sentiment to which Henry can definitely relate.

Henry lifts his eyes to a heaven that is clothed in the swath of light that is our galaxy, and he remembers how myths from all over the world and from the dim recesses of memory have given the Milky Way its name and have explained its origin. The Greeks believed it was created when suckling Heracles dribbled the breast milk of Hera, the wife of Zeus, across the evening sky. It was also described as the trail to Mount Olympus, the home of the Gods, and as the path of ruin made by the chariot of the Sun God Helios. In Sanskrit, the Milky Way was called Akash Ganga, or Ganges of the Heavens, and was thought to be sacred. Hindu cosmology describes the galaxy as an ocean of milk that was churned by the gods for a thousand years to release Amrita, the nectar of immortal life. To Henry's uncomplicated mind, it has probably been a little bit of all these things.

The adventures described within the pages of The Lost Journal of Huckleberry Henry are a "work in progress" because to those of us who have read these entries, it seems that it has not been the destination, but rather the journey, that has been important to Henry. Maybe the sand on the beaches of his life was meant to be swept away from time to time into unexplored oceans, and then to be deposited upon distant shores. Maybe Henry has been allegorically privileged thereby to discover the heretofore unknown possibilities of existence. As Brutus told Cassius: "There is a tide (after all) which taken at the flood, leads on to fortune. Omitted, all the voyage of (our lives) is bound in shallows and in miseries. On such a full sea are we now afloat, and we must take the current when it serves, or lose our ventures." (Shakespeare).

Upon his passport to life, Henry's five somatic senses have left indelible stamps that witness his wild adventures in the wilderness below the Selkirk Crest. After that fateful day picking huckleberries in the dense patches below the Wigwams, thoughts of survival occupied Henry's mind as weeks merged into months, and months into years. In the process, though, his brain has become a powerful blender that has whisked the sensations of bird calls, the howling of wolves, the scream of eagles, the whistling of the wind, the crack of thunder up on the Crest, and even the brooding silence of winter evenings, into frothy virgin piña colatas of perception. In time, these have become his windows on the world, and he has genuinely begun to enjoy the view. The recipe from which the concoction of his experiences has been made is proprietary, but its ingredients are anything but tedious. On the contrary, his wilderness adventures have become the foundation of zesty signature specialty drinks complete with little paper umbrellas that have fortified him against the rain that has inevitably fallen on many of his parades. Occasionally, he is delighted to find these libations topped with the empirical equivalents of mouthwatering cherries to hold his interest and with whipped cream that keep him coming back asking for more, please!

Mother Nature is hard on those who tempt fate by constructing "home improvements" in the North Idaho Panhandle. Each year, She seems to delight in wreaking havoc on both Henry and his homestead. But he just puts his nose to the grindstone and does his best to restore himself and his humble abode to their prior condition, only to see a repeat performance the following spring. It seems that he is engaged in a never-ending battle that can never be won. But that may be Her point. Perhaps inadvertently (or perhaps intentionally) She gives Henry the power "to do", and each year, when he responds to that prompting, he is intangibly added upon in ways that would have been difficult to duplicate, even if, in Her divine design, She had blessed him with other talents in different circumstances.

How many times, late on a summer evening, after the crowds have gone back to their campsites, has Henry lingered on the beach at Indian Creek, Squaw Bay, or Mosquito Bay, to look up at the sky, to inhale the aether of the stars twinkling in the heavens? He does it out of sheer joy, for on many occasions, he has caught angels in the celestial city of God winking at him.

Despite the efforts of revisionist historians and misguided government bureaucrats to remove the term "Squaw" from geographical locations throughout the United States, Squaw Bay at Priest Lake remains unscathed. The reality is that historically the term "squaw" was simply used as a general word for an indigenous woman. It was not a racial slur nor was it derogatory to women, in general. For example, the Massachusetts Bible, printed in 1663 used the word "squa" as a translation of the word "female", and of the words "younger women." In 1662, in the Plymouth Colony, the words "squa sachem" refer to the wife of the chief, with the connotation that she was esteemed as a "queen." As is the case with many other terms, it could be argued that the word "squaw" has only recently become offensive, coincident with the advent of politically correct language and of overzealous social justice warriors who are always looking for a new cause upon which to squander their energy. (Sorry for using the term "warrior." I hope that is still okay.)

It has not been lost on Henry's philosopher side to recognize that the ceaseless wave action pounding the beaches of Priest Lake changes their shape, size, and composition. At one time, the breakers may bring in new sand, and at another, sweep away that which had previously been deposited. The only constant is that of change. Henry is an actor, and he will only briefly grace the world's stage and feel the sand between his toes on the beaches of his life. When he has mastered the part he has been asked to play, and when he has successfully faced the wind and the waves to the best of his ability, he, like the rest of us, will move on to embrace both new and challenging opportunities. He will be the better for having fully immersed himself within a personalized curriculum that has been designed to expand with his increasing capabilities to infinite proportion.

Huckleberry Henry doesn't need Mother Nature to prompt him to recognize that he is not alone in the universe. A kindred spirit who also pushed the boundaries of human experience penned lines that would have resonated with Henry: "The Earth rolls upon her wings, and the Sun giveth his light by day, and the Moon giveth her light by night, and the stars also give their light, as they roll upon their wings in their glory, in the midst of the power of God. Behold, all these are kingdoms, and any (one) who hath seen any or the least of these hath seen God moving in his majesty and power." (Joseph Smith).

Henry's Lost Journal bears witness to the transformation of his rough and undisciplined nature, so much so that those who read his entries have been struck by their similarity to the expressions of William Mulock. In different circumstances, but embracing a similar philosophy, Mulock remained at work with his hands on the plough and his face to the future. Even as the shadows of evening lengthened about him, the morning was always in his heart. He knew, as Henry has come to realize, that the castle of enchantment is always before us, allowing us to catch daily glimpses of its battlements and its towers. The best of life is always further on, and will only briefly be hidden from our eyes, existing as it does, somewhere beyond the hills of time.

Huckleberry Henry is fortunate to have retained his faith, given the harsh and unrelenting austerity of his day-to-day living conditions. In his previous life, he had seen the awful grip of darkness enslave those who had refused to acknowledge the magical light that steadily pulsed from within the jewels that had been scattered by Providence across the beaches of their lives. Because his contemporaries had failed to recognize these love letters sent from God, their habitations had eventually become desolate, forlorn, and forsaken, as Nature withheld her bounties. Henry has determined that he will not allow himself to repeat his own mistakes or befall their fate. He knows that if he does not remain diligent, but alienates himself from Nature, all the world will become his enemy, and he will be left to fight his battles alone, without the Providential intervention that he has come to rely upon.

No matter how powerfully the winds of adversity might blow, or how fiercely the tempests of the adversary might attempt to undermine the principles that have buttressed the breastwork of his faith, Huckleberry Henry remains confident that he has done what he can to fortify his little patch of heaven in No Telley Basin, somewhere between Smith Peak and Lost Creek. He may not realize it, but it is equally true that by doing so, he has anchored himself to the Infinite.

Henry's wilderness hideaway has become a sanctuary where he can broaden his perspective, extend his depth of field, and lift his eyes to strain beyond the limited horizon of his vision. The solid foundation beneath his feet allows him to be cast off into the stream of an inspirational expansion of knowledge. Protected from the influence of the raging storms sweeping over the world, he has been carried along in the quickening currents of an intimate experience with the Cosmos.

Henry's most accurate and reliable direction finder is right over his head. It is Polaris, the North Star, so named because it sits over the North Pole. When he finds it in the night sky, he is oriented to true north to within 1.3°. Anyone who has spent any time in the woods has gotten lost or has at least become disoriented. Most of the time, it's a simple question of pausing, taking a deep breath, and consulting a map. On occasion, however, it becomes more complicated than that. When it's getting dark, or if you are fatigued, cold, or incapacitated in any way, you might not be as sharp as you normally would be. It gets even worse if you are without a compass or chart. How do you find true north, and ultimately, the way back to the safety of your camp? Henry has learned that prominent among several options is the Shadow Stick Method, (that unfortunately, works only on a sunny day.) He places a stick vertically in the ground and marks the tip of its shadow with a small stone. After 20 minutes, he marks the tip of the shadow again with another stone. When he scribes a line between the two, voila! - it points east - west. And, as a bonus, in the Northern Hemisphere, south is in the direction of the stick.

The Shadow Stick Method works on a sunny day, but what about on a clear night? All Henry needs to do is look for the North Star, which is oriented in the sky at true north. It is the last star in the handle of the Little Dipper. If you can't find that, look for the Big Dipper. The outer stars of its cup point right to Polaris. The Big Dipper is low in the northeast sky at nightfall, but it will climb upward during the evening hours, to reach its zenith in the wee hours after midnight. Inasmuch as Henry is often out and about at this time scattering glitter for the Woodland Elves and distributing the necklaces they have made to children who are fast asleep in the Priest Lake State Park Campgrounds, the position of the North Star will often guide him first to the children, and then back to his cabin in the woods.

Earth's axis wobbles like a top, tracing out a circle over a 25,772-year period. This process, known as precession, causes its North Pole to point over time toward different parts of the sky. Polaris is currently our North Star out of pure coincidence and has been so for only the last few hundred years. It appears stationary in the sky because it is positioned close to the line of the Earth's axis above the pole as it is projected into space. As such, it's the only bright star whose position relative to our rotating Earth does not change over the course of a night. All the other stars appear to sweep opposite to the Earth's rotation beneath them. However, the North Star is still offset by about 0.65° from celestial north, due to precession. Therefore, Polaris is technically not stationary in the sky; it scribes a very small circle every 24 hours, but it's only an imperceptible 1.3° in diameter. That's not nearly enough of a deviation to throw Henry off when, for example, he is looking for a particular cabin in a particular bay and needs to determine true north to find it.

Another way for Henry to find Polaris is to "follow the gaze of the moon." It "faces" the pointer stars lined up along the outer edge of the cup of the Big Dipper. Once they are located, Henry shifts his own scrutiny from the pointer stars to find the first star in the handle of the Little Dipper. As the Earth turns, every other star appears to spin around its axis, tracing out a circle in the sky, but the North Star seems to stand still. No matter the time of night or the season of the year, following Polaris will lead Henry due north. It's like following Peter Pan's instruction to Wendy, when he was describing to her how she could confidently navigate to Neverland through a sea of stars. "Take the first star on the right and go straight on 'til morning." He explained: "All you need is pixie dust and a little faith, and you can fly." That said, Henry has found that Elven glitter is an acceptable substitute for pixie dust.

Henry can also deduce north by simply observing the Milky Way Galaxy. Viewed from the Selkirks, it rises in the southeast, crosses the southern horizon, and then sets in the southwest. There is a good chance of seeing the core of the galaxy from anywhere south of 55° north. Above that latitude, it will never rise above the horizon. At Priest Lake, our Galactic Center is clearly visible from March to October, and the optimum season for viewing is in the summer when the Sun is on the opposite side of the sky, as long as hot, stormy, cloudy weather, or short nights don't disrupt opportunities. The Milky Way's core isn't easily visible for the rest of the months of the year because its orientation is close to the Sun. On dark, clear nights, however, Henry can easily observe the lack of stars in the broad band of wispiness that is a characteristic of the Milky Way. But that dark void isn't what you'd think; it's not due to an absence of stars, but instead to an immense galactic cloud of inky dust that, from our perspective, obscures the individual stars of the Milky Way.

But what must also be factored into the observation of the Milky Way are the location and phase of the Moon and artificial light pollution. Generally, the dense part of the Milky Way is best viewed when it is as high as possible in the southern sky. During April and May, the pre-dawn hours are best. From June to early August, the best time is near midnight, though the Milky Way will be visible almost all night long. From mid August through September, the best time is as soon as the sky has grown dark after sunset. Looking toward the Milky Way during the summer concentrates our gaze at the glowing line that defines the center of the galaxy, as seen from the spiral arm where Earth is located. In the springtime, when the Earth is on the other side of the Sun within the solar system, we look up at the sky in the opposite direction, away from the galactic center. It doesn't help that the Milky Way is also almost coincident with the horizon, and therefore is nearly invisible to our eyes.

Another method for finding north relies on moss. In the Northern Hemisphere, it tends to grow more abundantly on the north side of tree trunks, not to mention the roofs of cabins at Priest Lake. But Henry must be careful when using this method, for it isn't foolproof. In addition, in the Northern Hemisphere, deciduous trees tend to grow on the south side of hills, while evergreens grow on the north side. Another technique involves pushing two sticks of different lengths into the ground, with their tips lined up on any bright star in the night sky for reference. Any star will do. If it moves up over time, you are facing east toward No Telley Basin; down, and you are facing west toward the Twin Islands; right, and you are facing south toward Coolin; left, and you are facing north toward Five Mile Ridge.

Within the Milky Way, the Zodiac is composed of the 12 signs of a horoscope. It is closely tied to the Earth's motion in relation to the Sun. The signs are derived from the 12 major constellations that mark the path that the Sun appears to take as it moves across the sky throughout the year. In fact, there are 88 recognized constellations. All are clusters of stars within the Milky Way that are grouped together in particular patterns and have been given names. The constellations of the Zodiac are Aquarius, Aries, Cancer, Capricorn, Gemini, Leo, Libra, Pisces, Sagittarius, Scorpio, Taurus, and Virgo. These constellations were first named by the Babylonians, who integrated them into a two-dimensional star chart. For millennia, this map of the Zodiac has proven to be very useful for observers who have wished to track the movement of the solar system and the stars throughout the course of a year. It made life easier for ancient astronomers to find objects and determine their location in the sky, as well as for sailors, who used the stars to plot their own position on the high seas. The twelve constellations of the Zodiac lie along an elliptic plane as seen from Earth, defined by the circular path that the Sun appears to follow across the sky. In effect, the Sun seems to pass through these constellations over the course of a year, and because of its predictable cyclical journey through the Zodiac, ancient cultures were able to determine the seasons of the year. In a similar way, Henry uses the Zodiac as his own rough calendar.

Tucked in the flyleaf of Henry's Lost Journal were a few more of his favorite motivational quotes: The mountain man is not intimidated, but rather is inspired, by the mountains. ..... A mountain man is not discouraged by problems; instead, he is challenged by them. ..... Mountains were created to be conquered, adversities were designed to be defeated, and problems have been given to mountain men to be solved. .....Your doubt can create problems, but your faith can move mountains. ..... By far, I would rather die on a mountainside than in bed. ..... All I need is a mountain breeze and tall trees. ..... Sometimes, you just need a mountain to cleanse the bitter taste of disappointment from your soul. ..... If you think adventure in the mountains is dangerous, try routine. It can be lethal.

Henry has survived in the wilderness for a long time, and has not yet plumbed the depths of his abilities as a mountain man. However, he knows that potential energy is linked to position, while kinetic energy is related to motion. In anticipation of the opportunities that the new dawn might bring, he consciously prepares himself to be ready to answer the call whenever it might come, and then to confidently move forward with purpose, having accurately determined his position within the trail system of the Selkirks.

During the day, sunlight infuses our atmosphere, with reflected and refracted beams coming at us from all directions, but light pollution is an insidious problem that is growing at an alarming rate. A glaring example is Las Vegas, Nevada, which, from space, is the brightest city on earth. (Pyongyang, North Korea, is the darkest.) Excessive brightness (glare), brightness over inhabited areas (skyglow), unintended or unneeded light (light trespass), and bright and excessive groupings of light sources (clutter or over-illumination) interrupt sleep and confuse the circadian rhythm that guides day and night activities and affects physiological processes in nearly all living organisms. Light pollution contributes to climate change, washes out starlight in the night sky, disrupts ecosystems, and wastes energy. In general, most of America's remaining pristine night skies are concentrated in rural parts of the West. At one time or another, Henry has witnessed all the manifestations of light pollution, particularly when thoughtless cabin owners leave exterior lights burning through the night. Fortunately, Priest Lake rarely experiences significant light pollution. Together with all its friends, Henry would like to keep it that way.

One third of the world's population and 80% of Americans can no longer see the Milky Way. Light pollution is a global problem, and not just for humans. Fireflies, for instance, have gradually reduced in number and in some places have completely disappeared because of bright artificial light at night. Birds migrating at night, among other nocturnal animals, have become disoriented after being misdirected by bright skies that are the unintended consequence of artificial light. Of the few remaining pristine skies that are concentrated in rural parts of the American West, Priest Lake consistently makes the list when it comes to the best places for viewing the Milky Way and the Northern Lights in the lower 48 states. Above its canopy of larch, Douglas fir, cedar, and hemlock within the Idaho Panhandle National Forest, it is a tranquil night sky sanctuary. Its remote location, tucked as it is among the Selkirk, Cabinet, Coeur d'Alene, Purcell, and Bitterroot mountain ranges, makes North Idaho the gold standard for stargazing, in Huckleberry Henry's humble opinion.

It hasn't taken Huckleberry Henry very long to figure out that there is something about his interaction with Nature that has bound his own heartbeats to the majestic rhythm of the Cosmos. Countless times during his years in the woods, Henry has stood in awe of the power and majesty of the God of Nature, Whose thunder and lightning storms have wheeled across the lake, streaked over his head, and splashed and crashed above him along the Selkirk Crest. From Bible School days, Henry remembers David's experience when the Lord manifested His heavenly glory: "Fire (went) before (Him and) enlightened the world. The earth saw, and trembled. The hills melted like wax at the presence of the Lord of the whole earth." (Psalms 97:3-5).

Endless creative possibilities are catalyzed in Henry's mind by the summer storms that pound the shores of Priest Lake before rolling over the ridges high up on the Crest. He recalls a multitude of questions that he had never before thought to ask, and as he dangles his feet over the edges of granite slabs, his senses are overwhelmed with understanding. As he ventures into undiscovered country North of The Narrows of his mind, expanding awareness enlarges his comprehension to unprecedented proportion. Over the noise and the tumult, if he listens very intently, he can hear what God is thinking.

It has been a pitched battle between Huckleberry Henry and Mother Nature, one in which neither of them has conceded defeat nor claimed victory. Those who have read the accounts in Henry's Lost Journal have concluded that they've wrestled to a draw. They recall the counsel of Teddy Roosevelt, who declared of individuals like Henry: "It is far better to dare mighty things, even though checkered by failure, than to close ranks with those who neither enjoy much nor suffer much because they live within a gray twilight that knows neither victory nor defeat." ("The Strenuous Life"). It is in that spirit that we might charitably judge Henry, think positively of his efforts, and wish him well, even if he sometimes appears to joust with windmills.

It is Huckleberry Henry's cheerful good nature that has allowed him to discover the tiny flecks of gold within the detritus of life, and then to recognize the silver lining of celestial origin that surely exists in every sow's ear. Henry is a self-educated man, and he often recalls a few lines of prose that he memorized when he lived down below. Little did he think it would give him solace later in life during his trying times in the wilderness. ""My life is but a weaving between the Lord and me," the poet had written. "I cannot choose the colors, and yet He worketh steadily. Oft-times, He weaveth sorrow, and I, in foolish pride, forget that He seeith the upper, and I, the underside. Not 'til the loom is silent, and the shuttles cease to fly, shall God unroll the canvas and explain the reasons why. The dark threads are as needful in the Weaver's skillful hand as the threads of gold and silver in the pattern He has planned." (Benjamin Malachi Franklin).

Huckleberry Henry firmly believes that if you've been given a lemon, it is your God-given responsibility to find the recipe for lemonade (and then possibly sell it at the curb to passersby for 5 cents a glass). He also believes in playing the hand you've been dealt, in taking whatever ingredients that are at your disposal and, instead of eating left-overs out of a tin can, creating a sumptuous five-course meal. With his positive mental attitude, Henry has learned to keep tempests in teapots where they belong, and to put all things in perspective. He retains the joyful anticipation of the optimistic little boy, who, when faced with the daunting task of shoveling up an enormous pile of manure from a horse stall near his home, enthusiastically set about his task with the exclamation: "There's got to be a pony in there somewhere!"

Huckleberry Henry is a work in progress and his magnum opus is unfinished. During his life in the wilderness, the list of the things that could go wrong has been frustratingly long. In fact, he has concluded, it is probably endless. Henry measures twice and cuts once, and yet he still comes up with a short board from time to time. But he understands well and has been guided in life by this principle: Until we are dedicated to a worthy cause, "there is hesitancy, the chance to draw back, and always ineffectiveness. Concerning acts of initiative, there is one elementary truth, the ignorance of which kills countless ideas and splendid plans, and it is this: The moment we commit ourselves, then Providence moves too. All sorts of things fall into place to help us that would never have otherwise occurred. A whole stream of events issues from the decision, raining down in our favor all manner of unforeseen assistance that we could not have beforehand dreamed would have come our way." (Thomas F. Hornbein).

For Huckleberry Henry, living in the wilderness has been a dangerous proposition, with a strong likelihood of accident or injury at a moment when he least expects it. But he has learned that even his wounds serve a purpose, for they have become the portals through which light has entered him. In his former life, Henry had been a Trekkie, and he still remembers how Q had warned Captain Jean Luc Picard: "You judge yourselves against the pitiful adversaries you've encountered so far - mountain lions and wolves. They're nothing compared to what's waiting. You are about to move into areas of the Selkirk wilderness containing wonders more incredible than you can possibly imagine, and terrors to freeze your soul." Later in the same episode, after a particularly traumatic encounter with an angry grizzly sow with cubs, Q warned Picard: "If you can't take a little bloody nose, maybe you ought to go back to your cabin and crawl under your bed. It's not safe out here. It's wondrous, with treasures to satiate desires both subtle and gross, but it's not for the timid."

Huckleberry Henry has adapted to the slower pace of life that, arguably, has been perfected by Priest Lake's residents. He doesn't rush into things, but instead lets each day unfold before him. He has learned to pause, to weigh his options, to think, to look around, to enjoy his interaction with Nature, and to let its harmony infuse him with a zest for living that stimulates affirmative action. He has embarked upon a vision quest that has become a ceremonial rite of passage, with its attendant opportunities for solitude and fasting. By affirming his inner strength, he is better prepared to face his fears. His experiences in the wilderness have prepared him to awaken his spirit, heal his body, and transform his soul.

Huckleberry Henry doesn't feel sorry for himself, and as we read his Journal entries, we mustn't lose faith in him. On the margin of one of its pages, he penned a line from the memoirs of Helen Keller, whom he considered a fellow coureur des bois: "Dark as my path may seem, I carry a magic light in my heart. Faith, the spiritual strong searchlight, illuminates the way. Although sinister doubts lurk in the shadow, I walk unafraid toward the Enchanted Wood where the foliage is always green, where joy abides, nightingales nest and sing, and where life and death are one in the presence of our Creator."

Sometimes, on sultry August days beneath Mount Roothaan, at Indian Creek, Shipman Point, Nordman, and the Stagger Inn, it gets so hot, Huckleberry Henry has seen his dog chasing a squirrel, and both were walking. It gets so hot, his chickens lay fried eggs; so hot his iceberg lettuce has melted; so hot, he once saw a bee take off its yellow jacket; so hot, he can wash and dry his clothes at the same time; so hot, he starts wearing sweat pants; so hot that he has seen birds using oven mitts to pull worms out of the ground; and so hot his campfire has lighted itself. The simple answer to why it gets hot in the summer is that the Sun shines longer. Its rays also hit the Earth at a steeper angle in the summer and thereby pass through less atmosphere. This increases the amount of solar energy focused on the area of the Earth that is tilted toward the sun, contributing to hotter temperatures.

Huckleberry Henry has several essential items on his wish-list. One is a genuine mattress for the bed in his one-room cabin. He admits that choosing the style has been a big decision, not to be approached lightly or quickly consummated. "I need to sleep on it," he wrote in his Journal.

Henry enjoys hiking up to the granite cirques that dot the Selkirk Crest. He is generally unaware that they were formed by ice and mark the heads of long-gone hanging glaciers that scoured out their characteristic bowl shapes. Often, lakes formed at the base of these geologic deformations after the ice had melted. Henry can see examples of this at Two Mouth Lakes, Hunt Lake, Fault Lake, Harrison Lake, Myrtle Lake, McCormack Lake, Caribou Lake, Pyramid Lake, Roman Nose Lake, and Beehive Lake. The granite cirques of the Selkirks provide Henry with a firm foundation for looking up at the stars. As he does so, he discerns the "fire-folk sitting in the air in bright boroughs and circled citadels." (Gerald Hopkins, "The Starlight Night").

Living in the woods has endowed Huckleberry Henry with spiritual enlightenment that has created a celestial bridge transporting him past the improbabilities of life to the stability of understanding, not only of this world, but also of the eternal realm that lies just beyond the far horizon. Fire in the sky is the sure witness of its reality.

One of the things Henry has gotten quite good at is identifying deer. Ear size, tail shape, antlers, and other features and behavior help him distinguish between muleys and whitetail deer. Muleys get their name from their overly large ears, while whitetails get theirs from the opposite end. However, most of the time, on the rump of a mule deer you see larger patches of white, which are only partly covered by a rope-like, white tail with a black tip. Whether the tail is up or down, you can always see plenty of white on the rear-end of a mule deer. A whitetail, on the other hand, only raises its tail to reveal its white underside when it wants to alert others in the herd of danger. As an effective defense mechanism, the difference between "calm" and "freaked out" is as big as possible, and Henry has no trouble identifying whitetail deer that are running away from him.

Muleys tend to be a bit bigger than whitetails, but age, nutrition and other environmental factors play big roles in determining their height and weight. Bucks of both species shed their antlers yearly - in January or February for whitetails, while mule deer typically shed theirs in February or March. Mature mule deer racks are taller and broader than those of whitetails. They are also bifurcated, meaning they fork in two directions as they grow, splitting to create more points. A whitetail buck's antlers all grow off one main beam. With proper nutrition, older bucks of both species generally have larger antlers with more points than do younger deer. Like muleys, whitetails have dichromatic (two color) vision, with blue and yellow being the primaries. Thus, deer can only poorly distinguish orange and red, which makes it convenient for hunters to wear brightly colored gear in the woods.

Across their range, whitetails are highly variable in size. Bucks stand about three feet tall, weighing around 130 - 220 pounds, but in rare cases, bucks over 400 pounds have been recorded in the northernmost reaches of the Panhandle. Muleys are slightly larger than whitetails, standing three to three and a half feet tall at the shoulder, with bucks weighing 125 - 250 pounds, but a trophy buck can weigh in at more than 450 pounds.

The face of a muley is mostly white from the nose to the eyes, whereas the whitetail's face is mostly brown with white rings around its eyes and nose. Both have a white patch on their throats. The distinctive large ears of the muley tend to be set at about a 30° angle on the head, versus those of whitetails, which are rounded and stand more erect. Mule deer have grayish-brown fur, whereas whitetail fur is usually more reddish-brown. However, whitetails get more gray in the winter, which makes color differentiation unreliable. When running, whitetails gallop, rather than hop, whereas muleys have a stiff-legged, bounding hop, which Huckleberry Henry can relate to, since his lumbago has been flaring up lately.

Unlike Henry's dog, whitetails only wag their tails when they are startled. They have a very long stride of up to 25 feet when running, can reach 30 miles per hour, and can jump 8 feet, even though they are smaller than muleys. They live four or five years in the wild, although 2017 saw almost 3 million whitetail bucks in varying stages of maturity harvested throughout the United States. Both species normally poop easily identifiable dark brown to black pellets about a half inch in diameter.

Whitetail does can breed during their first fall at only 6 months of age. Henry thinks that's a little weird, but he has decided it's fruitless to argue with Mother Nature over trivialities. She has her ways. Mule deer take longer to mature, and mate from mid to late November; whitetails breed from late November to early December. Gestation for both species is around 6 months. Both deliver one to four fawns (normally two) in late May or early June. A doe will usually produce a single fawn the first year and then twins subsequently. The fawns are reddish with white spots for camouflage, and weigh about 6 pounds at birth. They nurse within the first hour and stand within the first 12 hours. During their first weeks, they see their mothers only at mealtime, but they'll stay with the doe for the first full year. Their spots will begin to fade by the end of their first month.

The winter coats of both muleys and whitetails have hollow guard hairs over a furry undercoat that helps retain body heat. The are so well insulated that not even enough heat escapes to melt the snow on their backs, so, if you happen to be concerned for their welfare during the winter, as Henry was at first, rest assured that they don't feel the cold or the snow.

Henry wonders about the deer who are destined to live out their lives in the woods at the mercy of the elements, while he has been fortunate to be able to hunker down under his blanket in his snug little cabin on cold winter nights. His thoughts have turned to the hand that fate has dealt him. In Greek mythology, the Fates were Clotho, who spun the thread of life, Lachesis, who chose our lot in life and measured how long it was to be, and Atropos, who at our death would cut the thread of life with her shears. In Henry's case, the Fates have been inexorably stitched into the fabric of his personal history, like the Book of Kells or the Bayeux Tapestry. When he stops to think about fate, Henry is overwhelmed by both its simplicity and its importance. It is in the armory of his thoughts that he has fashioned the tools to deal with the exigencies of the day, and then, with his words he has shaped condition. Finally, with his deeds, he has influenced environment and destiny. It could be argued that he has tempted the Fates with his words, thoughts, and deeds, and that if he has not emerged the victor, he has at least reached a deterministic accommodation with them.

Each morning, as Henry sets out on his day's journey, he takes a few deep breaths of a celestial aether that invigorates him as would North Idaho nitrous oxide. He partakes of its rapid transformations, its active enchantment reaches his dust, and his lungs dilate as he conspires with the morning wind. (See R.W. Emerson). Henry plots his course, plans his work, and works his plan. He reconnoiters the path he will follow for potential dangers and pre-plays before he re-plays, rehearsing how he will respond to perilous situations. He has scouted the rapids in the river of life and knows where the rocks are hidden within its swift current. He knows how large each cataract is, how deep the holes are, and where he will encounter shallow pools for quiet respite. He has learned where he will be able to grasp the horns of sanctuary to recuperate and clear his head before another challenge presents itself just around the next bend in the river.

As Henry contemplates the stars wheeling across the night sky, he arrives at an epiphany relating to opposition in all things. He realizes that the universe, that has been spread out before him in the panorama of the Milky Way, is so well balanced that the very fact that he has challenges suggests that there are solutions yet to be discovered, and there are untapped sources of energy that are waiting to be applied to his benefit.

Henry realizes that if butterflies didn't need to struggle to free themselves from their cocoons, they would never fly. If sea turtles didn't run the gauntlet from the warm sandy nests in which they were born to the water's edge, they might never experience the exhilaration of swimming with sharks and other predators. If squirrels didn't busily gather acorns before winter's long night, they would quickly starve to death. If bears didn't fatten up on spawning salmon and on huckleberries before lumbering off into hibernation, they might wither away to (almost) nothing, while dreaming of pots of honey as they slumbered in their dens. If Huckleberry Henry hadn't been required to scratch out his living hour by hour and day by day, by the sweat of his brow and the labor of his hands, he would have shriveled up long ago and quietly died on the vine, even as the bounty of the earth crowded all about him.

In the wildebeest migration through the Serengeti Plain of Masai National Park, vast herds cross the Mara River in a desperate gamble that they will be among the lucky ones to make it to the far bank without being eaten by a crocodile. Nature has endowed each of them with a shot of adrenaline that compels them to unhesitatingly jump off the bank and take the risk. In the Selkirks, when Henry encounters equally terrifying swollen rivers in front of him, with unseen dangers lurking in their depths, he adjusts the heavy burdens on his back in preparation to meet the challenge before him. He realizes that he will sink or swim largely on his own. He hopes and prays for "the serenity to accept the things he cannot change, the courage to change the things he can, and the wisdom to know the difference." (Reinhold Niebuhr).

By now, readers will surely have noticed that many pages in Huckleberry Henry's Lost Journal have been devoted to deer, elk, and moose. As had been the case when he lived down below, in the woods Henry continues to spend a lot of time observing them and gathering their sheds. He is in good company. Cave paintings and ceremonial objects dating from prehistoric times have incorporated antlers into rituals of cultural importance, and clearly illustrate that they are a renewable resource. Each spring, male members of North America's deer family grow a new pair after shedding the old ones at the end of winter. Female mountain caribou also follow this pattern in the far north. Even more amazing is the fact that in the peak of summer, as new antlers make their stubby appearance, a bull elk can grow an inch of antler and a deer can grow a half inch of antler daily. They are the fastest growing bone found in nature. Theories abound as to why members of the deer family shed their antlers, with no definitive answer forthcoming. Some things are just meant to be, for the enjoyment of the bearers as well as for the observers and hunters.

Breeding plays a major role in antler shedding with a direct link to testosterone. Generally, larger, dominant bucks drop their antlers earlier in the winter than their younger brethren who are kept away from the festivities. Researchers have tested this theory by penning bucks separately from does and prohibiting breeding. The "pent up" bucks, not expending testosterone, kept their antlers up to two months longer than their party brethren who were free to breed at will. Henry has made a mental note of this.

Antlers typically exhibit character, as no two are ever the same. When and where an animal sheds its antlers will vary with geography, environment, and the age of the deer, elk, or moose. Drought, moisture, cold, heat, and predation directly influence their health and stress. but they all typically shed their antlers around the same window of time, year after year. Whitetails begin dropping theirs soon after the first of the year, although the majority drop in February and March. Rodents such as mice, squirrels, and porcupines, and even wolves, coyotes, and bears, chew on sheds because they are a source of calcium, sodium, phosphorus, magnesium, barium, iron, aluminum, zinc, strontium, and manganese. A rodent can gnaw an antler to a nub in a matter of weeks, and spring ground cover can quickly hide antlers in the burgeoning flora.

Sheds are typically found in south-facing bedding areas consisting of thick cover, where animals spend most of their day resting and hiding from predators. They also go there to soak up the warmth of ambient sunlight during the day, for the low-lying browse that is available, and, at night, to take advantage of protection from the elements. Deer, moose, and elk tend to bed in tall grass, brushy thickets, and heavily wooded pockets of timber, preferring slopes exposed to the most sunlight, where they can absorb heat to preserve energy. Branches in conifer thickets block the wind and catch snow before it hits the ground. Also, it's almost impossible for a predator to sneak up on a deer and launch a surprise attack when it must navigate tangles of briars and dry, fallen branches. Shedding begins a month or two after the rut, about the same time that bucks, depleted from its rigors, are seeking out concentrated food sources. Henry always looks for dips, depressions, heads of ravines, low spots shielded from prevailing winds, and travel corridors leading away from food and toward those dense bedding areas. As the days draw closer to an animal dropping its rack, the antlers will loosen up. So, Henry looks for any place where they might have had to jump across or over something that could have jarred their head.

By early April, most deer will have shed their antlers, although on rare occasions some have been seen carrying their intact racks into May. Southern exposure, whether it be the face of a hill or edge of a forest where it meets a clearing, provides thermal radiation for members of the deer family. Because these areas soak up sunlight, they often are a few degrees warmer than the northern edge of the same cover, and they often retain less snow cover because of more rapid snow melt earlier in the spring. Lone evergreens seem to attract deer, and they'll go out of their way to bed under them, whether it's one pine in an overgrown field or just a few scattered trees in a hardwood forest. And more than 90 percent of the time, when a deer sheds antler under a single evergreen, it's on the southern side of the tree. When Henry finds one shed, he always looks for the second, typically between 50 and 100 yards away.

Dogs instinctively sniff out interesting treasures in the woods, so using one to find shed antlers makes sense. Shed hunting has grown so much in popularity that dogs are now trained specifically to search out and retrieve sheds, like a bird dog finds quail. Hours in the woods with a shed hunting dog is time well spent. They'll follow trails into thick cover and scan beds and south facing areas where deer seek refuge from late winter weather. While targeting feeding fields, Henry and his dog get on high ground, looking for antler tips or shiny spots of white. He knows that whether chased by a coyote or simply looking for a better sanctuary to ride out a storm, deer often go out of bounds. He and his dog will follow trails through briar thickets, willow stands and into cattail swamps, that often give up the best antlers because savvy, mature bucks often retire to these locations to escape confrontations with predators.

The most successful shed hunters look for tines, beams, and the general shapes and colors of antlers. Henry often will see just the tip of a tine poking through the snow or out of the mud. There are many ways he uses shed antlers, varying from turning them into tools to using them for décor. But he also simply enjoys the hunt and being outdoors. Sheds can also tell a big game hunter a lot about animal behavior. In some cases, Henry has tracked the growth of a deer by finding his sheds over several seasons. This helps him piece together his hunting strategy. Henry has also heard of those who hunt antlers for economic gain, who sell the sheds to collectors, naturopathic health specialists, furniture artisans, and other craftsmen.

The divine design of Henry's life is individually tailored to keep him moving faster, higher, and stronger: citius, altius, fortius! Maintaining his forward momentum sometimes compels him to hike throughout the night on forced marches without a break. But when doing so, he has the good fortune to brush up against the stars, and his reward is to be present at the dawn whose brilliance is dazzling. As his eyes make the adjustment, he is pleasantly surprised to see the world in a refreshingly new light, as it really is. He begins to feel the creative expression of powers that have always resided within him. That energy brings him closer to Nature, to a point where he can see beyond his cabin in No Telley Basin to envision his heavenly home. He is enveloped within the aroma of bread baking in a celestial oven, and he knows that one of the pans has his name on it.

Huckleberry Henry has adopted the work ethic of the Woodland Elves, and of the Seven Dwarfs who marched off each morning to toil in their diamond mine, loudly singing as they went: "Hi ho, hi ho, its off to work we go. We dig in our mine the whole day through. It is what we like to do." It may be that we who believe in fairies are the fortunate few, who like Henry, are the beneficiaries of the nightly endeavors of those gentle forest creatures who scatter, not only glitter, but also the jewels that magically reappear across the beaches of Southshores at Huckleberry Bay most mornings during the summer months, and especially when children are present.

Huckleberry Henry has spent enough time in the woods to become familiar with the location of the glitter mine of the Woodland Elves. Its whereabouts is a closely guarded secret, maintained for generations by the power of a blood oath. Nevertheless, Henry has gained the trust of the Elders in the Elf Council, and on the night of a blue moon, they leave a small leather pouch full of glitter on a prominent rock at a fork on the trail leading down from Five Mile Ridge to his cabin in No Telley Basin. Henry loves sprinkling pinches of sparkling glitter from the palm of his hand, and admiring how easily the flecks capture the light of the moonbeams. They seem to absorb a heavenly aura, and it dawns upon him that it is up to him to look for, and recognize, and then immerse himself within the spell of the Elves, so that it might wash over him and infuse him with a celestial energy. This gives him the courage to steal away from his solitude, descend to the campgrounds around the lake, and sprinkle glitter on the cheeks of the children who are fast asleep in their tents, so that when they awaken, they too might experience the euphoria of being overcome by the magical aether of Priest Lake.

Henry has always thought that there could be no better place to have a glitter mine than in the shadow of appropriately named Goblin Knob. Having said that, some say the Elves' mine must be in Long Canyon. Those holding that view cite the inaccessibility of that rift in the Selkirks that ranges from high peaks to low rainforest. The clear water of its stream runs unabated from the glaciated basins below the Selkirk Crest to a hanging valley above the Purcell Trench. It is the most remote place in North Idaho and is its largest valley without road access. Nestled beneath some of the highest peaks in the Selkirks, it boasts a spectacular stand of old growth western red cedar. In short, it is an ideal place for a working Elven glitter mine that would escape the attention of outsiders.

Henry, working beside the Elves, is certain that the jewels they cast into the waters of Priest Lake will survive the wind and waves for many years to come. In the meantime, they sparkle from within its pristine waters, conveying messages of hope to the tired and poor, to the huddled masses yearning to breathe free, and to the refuse that has been cast upon its inviting shoreline. These Henry welcomes, these lowlanders, the homeless and the tempest-tossed, with his lamp held high beside the golden door at the trailhead below No Telley Basin. (See Emma Lazarus, "The New Colossus").

Henry sometimes steals a few moments to walk along the lake at Southshores at Huckleberry Bay. He likes to do so because he occasionally finds one of the Elves' polished stones of red, green, yellow, or blue, hiding among the grains of sand. He wishes they might have been sapphires, rubies, emeralds, and diamonds, not for himself, but as treasures for the children whose excited voices he often hears on summer afternoons. In any case, he hopes to follow in the Elves' footsteps, that he might help to preserve and multiply the magic that has become synonymous with the experiences of so many at Priest Lake, which is, after all, the crown jewel of North Idaho.

Henry learns valuable lessons from his Elven friends as they scatter glitter and jewels across the beaches at Southshores, He notices that they save a few choice gems to be tossed into deep water, by design, intentionally creating demanding situations for those who seek them. In the process, the children of Priest Lake are challenged to dig deeply into their reserves as they exert real effort to retrieve the treasures. The Woodland Elves understand that in the conduct of the children's lives, they will be happiest, and will be most satisfied, only when they have expended soul sweat. With perspiration, they will be blessed with inspiration and will reach epiphanies. The charms they have been looking for will be revealed as pearls of great price.

The flickering light that is seen on summer evenings in the mountains above the lake is sometimes mistaken for heat lightning. But Henry's Lost Journal confirms that, on at least a few occasions, it has been something entirely different. He reports that at a recent Elven Convocation held in the shadow of Horton Ridge, his forest friends vividly taught him that a thousand points of light, when gathered together, cast a very large shadow. They further explained that if Henry would simply orient himself to the light, every apparition of danger would remain behind him. They revealed that one of the reasons why they are so active at night and during storms is because they have no reason to fear. The Elves have taken courage by embracing the light that is gathering in the East. And so, there is method in their madness. They take the jewels that they have polished and fling them across sandy beaches where their favorite children will find them. They know that the flickering light captured by some of these gemstones will surely catch the attention of those with sharp young eyes to brighten their darkest days. The Elves hope that some of the jewels might provide steady illumination for years to come and mark the way the children ought to go, as they journey along trails both familiar and unexplored beneath the Selkirk Crest.

The Elves have taught Huckleberry Henry that at some point, he will come to the end of the road and the Sun will slowly sink in the west behind Granite Mountain for the last time. But he has made it clear to them that he wants no rites in a gloom-filled room, for why should tears be shed for a soul that's been set free? Near the end of his Lost Journal is this poignant entry: "Miss me a little, but not too long, and not with your heads bowed low. Remember the times that we once shared; miss me, but let me go. For this is the journey we all must take, and each must go it alone. It's part of the Master's Plan for us, a step on the road back home. If you feel alone with heavy hearts, go to those we know, and reminisce about our good times. Miss me, but let me go." (Christina Rossetti).

It is not uncommon for children who have been taken on day hikes by their parents, to probe the boundaries of the Selkirks at Abandon Creek, Lion Creek, Two Mouth Creek, Indian Creek, Horton Creek, and Soldier Creek. They push into the cirques above Echo Bowl, Hunt Lake, McCormack Lake, and Caribou Lake. They make their way up Race Creek, beneath the lofty summits of Gunsight Peak and Mount Alasta. On more than one occasion, as families have lost their way after hours of boondocking through brush and timber, they have stumbled upon deserted Elven villages, hidden among the boulders lining the creeks. They have assumed the Elves were off working at their glitter mine, getting ready for another night of mischief.

After the Elves have been particularly active, glitter flickers in the sunlight amidst the forest duff, and Elven necklaces are sometimes discovered dangling from tree branches. Back at the Leonard Paul ice cream stand, at the soft-serve dispenser at Hills, and at the Indian Creek Store, it is easy to spot children who are eager to share stories of close encounters with both Elves and with Huckleberry Henry.

Children who have spent a great deal of time in the forest have been fortunate to stumble upon Elven icons every now and then. When they have carefully removed the excess moss and bark, they have been rewarded to behold the distinct images of Elves. Adults, however, often have difficulty discerning the resemblance. Their children often reassure their elders with words of encouragement, telling them that all they need is the faith to believe, and their eyes will be opened.

Encouraged by the discovery of these detailed wooden images of Elves, and incidentally, by what appear to be fair likenesses of Huckleberry Henry himself, campers have descended upon the woods all over the Selkirks in a quest to find evidence of the Elves and of Henry. Those elusive denizens of the forest have unintentionally generated something of a cult-following. Even casual huckleberry pickers (if there are, indeed, such things) have heard about Henry and the Elves, and have eagerly asked if they, too, might join in the search.

If we pay close attention to the exploits of the Woodland Elves, and to the escapades of Huckleberry Henry, it can be clearly seen that their joint mission is to save animals from needless exploitation from hunters and trappers, and to spare old growth forests from loggers who disrespect the land. Their sympathies are aligned with the less fortunate, who need the protection of others. Nature is hardly the villain, but is rather a worthy protagonist in the ongoing drama pitting the environment against the abuse of natural resources by the thoughtless, the careless, and the greedy.

During his meandering journey through time in North Idaho, Henry has been accompanied by over 300 wildlife species, including large animals like deer, elk, and moose, grizzly bears, black bears, mountain goats, and gray wolves, cougars, and coyotes, not to mention smaller ones like bald eagles, skunks, marten, river otters, beavers, lynx, and bobcats. Coeur d'Alene salamanders, pygmy shrews, garter snakes, and calliope hummingbirds, only help to make a small dent in the list.

Nine of Idaho's dozen big game animals can be found in the north country – whitetail and mule deer, elk, mountain goats, moose, black bears, grizzly bears, mountain lions, and wolves. (Pronghorn, and California and Rocky Mountain Bighorn sheep inhabit other parts of the state and complete the list). Huckleberry Henry is particularly careful when boondocking during hunting season. Because he prefers wearing his buckskins, he could easily be inadvertently mistaken for a deer by an overzealous hunter. In general, deer season is August 30 – December 24, elk season is August 1 – December 31, black bear seasons are April 1 – June 30, and August 30 – October 31, mountain lion season is August 30 – June 30, turkey season is August 30 – January 31, and wolf season is September 1 – March 31. There are also seasons in late summer and fall for rabbit, quail, partridge, pheasant, and squirrel. So, pretty much year-round, when he is hungry and his larder is empty, there is something in the woods trying to evade a bullet from Henry's 50 caliber Hawkin.

When Huckleberry Henry glasses animals in the Trapper Creek drainage, he often spots deer, elk, and moose, as well as a fair number of grizzlies and black bears prowling about on the opposite side of the valley. He sits quietly in the early hours of morning when the animals seem to be most active. Sometimes, the hair on the back of his neck stands up and he gets the odd feeling that he is not the only one who is doing the watching. The funny thing is, that when he hikes to the opposite side of the draw and glasses the area around the viewing platform where he had been only a half an hour before, he generally sees just as many animals in the thickets surrounding his former location.

Occasionally, Henry stumbles upon winter-kill, moose, elk, and deer that have succumbed to the unforgiving nature of the elements. Extreme cold temperatures and prolonged heavy snow cover can force them to expend energy and burn stored fat reserves at rates that strain their capacity. The main culprit of winter kill is prolonged cold weather that holds off the germination of vegetation. Their winter coats effectively absorb sunlight and trap body heat to provide needed protection from the cold, and oil-producing glands in their skin makes their hair water repellent. Their bodies retain more fat during the fall, and deer cut their metabolism in half during the winter by remaining less active and eating less. They hunker down during particularly harsh weather and may not move for days as they rely upon their stores of fat. They seek out areas that will provide wind resistance and cover, and with a good supply of twigs, stems, nuts, and mushrooms, they typically tolerate the passage to spring quite comfortably.

There is a lot of ground for Henry to cover in the Selkirks. In 1973, major portions of three national forests, the Kaniksu, Coeur d'Alene, and St. Joe were combined into the Idaho Panhandle National Forest, an area of timber spread out over two and a half million acres, with 4.7% in Eastern Washington and 1.2% in Western Montana. The Supervisor's Office is in Coeur d'Alene, with a district ranger office in Priest River, Idaho. This is Huckleberry Henry's stomping ground. It gives him elbow room and its size explains why he is so infrequently sighted. It also helps us to understand why, at his remote camp in No Telley Basin, surrounded by dozens of peaks of the Selkirk, Purcell, Cabinet, Coeur d'Alene, St. Joe, Clearwater, and Bitterroot Mountains, and under the canopy of thousands of stars, he sometimes feels insignificant. For perspective and a reality check, he has been known to pull his books prose of off the shelf in his cabin, turn the pages to "Ozymandias" and ponder his connection to its final lines: "My name is Ozymandias, (or Rameses), King of Kings. Look on my works, ye mighty, and despair! Nothing beside remains. Round the decay of that colossal wreck, boundless and bare the lone and level sands stretch far away." (Percy Bysshe Shelley).

From another of its pages, Washington Irving brooded: "It is the rule that history fades into fable; fact becomes clouded with doubt and controversy; the inscription moulders, and columns, arches, and pyramids are but heaps of sand, and their epitaphs, nothing but characters written in the dust." And yet, the Lost Journal of Huckleberry Henry stands as a shining example of a divine model that has been destined to reach at least a few intrepid souls who embrace the mountains of the Panhandle.

Huckleberry Henry has been blessed with plenty of time to ponder life's greatest questions, such as: What makes clouds float in the sky? After all, they are made of droplets of water or frozen crystals that are heavier than the air around them, so one would think that they would fall. But when the droplets are small, their motion generates friction with the air, so they have a harder time making their way down out of the cloud than their heavier counterparts. They're like tiny ice parachutes. In addition, updrafts of wind prevent small drops within the cloud from falling at all. In the end, the biggest drops fall first, from a rain cloud, followed by progressively smaller ones until there isn't enough water left to form more drops.

Not all clouds are created equally. Some are puffy, others are gray, or white, while others are so capricious that our minds start to see bunnies, turtles, or a nation's borders in their shapes. A cloud is a visible accumulation of minute droplets of water, ice crystals, or both, suspended in the air. Though they vary in shape and size, all are basically formed in the same way through the condensation of water vapor. When close to the ground, clouds are described as fog or mist. "There's a cloud on Henry's horizon of a wonderful shape and hue, like the feathery down of a snowdrift that's dimpled with changeful blue. He gazes on its shadowy outline and drinks in the calm of the skies, till he fancies it float out of heaven as an angel in disguise." (Kate McKinney).

The names of different types of clouds are based on their shape and how high up they float in the troposphere, which is the first and lowest layer of the Earth's atmosphere. It contains 75% of our planet's water vapor, and it is where most weather phenomena occur. Its average height is 10 miles. Often, the clouds within the troposphere are simply classified as cirrus, stratus, and cumulus because these are the most common and are representative of each altitude class. Cirrus clouds are feathery and are so high that they are made of ice particles. They portend fair weather when they are scattered in a clear blue sky. Stratus clouds look like flat white sheets that may stay put for several days. They can be harbingers of an overcast day, or they may bring rain. Cumulus clouds are puffy and look like balls of cotton. When they don't get very tall, they are indicators of fair weather. But when they do grow tall, although their bases are close to the ground, they morph into thunderstorms. All three of these classifications of clouds remain the "daughters of earth and water, and the nurslings of the sky. They pass through the pores of the ocean and shores; they change, but they cannot die. For after the rain when, with never a stain, the pavilion of Heaven is bare, and the winds and sunbeams with their convex gleam build up the blue dome of air, they silently laugh at their own (empty tombs,) and out of the caverns of rain, like children from the womb or ghosts from the tomb, they arise and (build up) again." (Percy Bysshe Shelley).

Cirrus is one of the most common types of clouds that are observed by Henry throughout the year. They're thin and wispy with a silky sheen. They're always composed of ice crystals whose degrees of separation determine how transparent they are. In addition to their filamentous appearance, cirrus clouds stand out among others because their crystals are often colored, through the refraction of light, in bright yellow or red before sunrise and after sunset, respectively. Cirrus clouds are the first to light up the sky in the morning and the last to fade away in the evening.

Cirrocumulus clouds are among the most gorgeous clouds out there. They usually form about two and a half miles above the ground with small white fluff that spreads out across the sky. They are called 'mackerel skies' because they can have a grayish color which makes them look a bit like fish scales. What's worth keeping in mind about cirrocumulus clouds is that they never generate rainfall, nor do they interact with other types of clouds to form larger patterns, but they can mean cold weather is in store.

Stratus clouds manifest themselves in thin layers that cover large areas of the sky. They form as mist when they are close to the ground. A stratus cloud is easily distinguished by long horizontal layers that have a fog-like appearance. They form within large masses of air that have risen in the troposphere and then condensed. They can produce light showers or even light snow, depending upon the ambient temperature. However, if enough moisture is retained at ground level, stratus clouds can transform into nimbostratus clouds (see below). Stratus clouds are very common, especially in coastal and mountainous regions, so Henry sees a lot of them in the Panhandle.

Cirrostratus clouds have a sheet-like wispy appearance that can look like a curly blanket covering the sky. They're quite translucent which makes it easy for the Sun or the Moon to peer through. Their color varies from light gray to white, and their fibrous bands can vary widely in thickness. Purely white cirrostratus clouds have stored moisture, indicating the presence of a warm frontal system. Some of the best cloud pictures involve cirrostratus clouds because their ice crystals beautifully refract light from the Sun or Moon, producing a dazzling halo effect. Cirrostratus clouds almost always move in a westerly direction, and their presence usually portends rainfall within 24 hours.

Nimbostratus clouds are heavy rain bearers with thick dark layers that completely block out the Sun. They form with the gradual accumulation of moisture over a large area within a warm frontal system that lifts moist air higher up into the atmosphere, where it then condenses. Nimbostratus clouds will generate a long steady rain.

Cumulus clouds are characterized by a white, fluffy appearance, resembling cauliflowers. They're the most recognizable of all the types of clouds. These 'piles of cotton' in the sky form large masses with well-defined rounded edges, which explains the name 'cumulus' which is Latin for 'heap'. Cumulus clouds are a sign of fair weather, although they may occasionally discharge rain in the form of light showers.

Altocumulus clouds are sometimes called 'social clouds' because they appear in groups. They have a grayish-white color with some portions darker than the others. They form at a lower altitude, so they're largely made up of water droplets. They are typically present between lower stratus clouds and higher cirrus clouds. When altocumulus clouds appear with another cloud type at the same time, stormy weather is usually in the forecast.

Stratocumulus clouds are low-lying and have a wide horizontal structure. They look like thick white blankets of stretched out cotton, and resemble cumulus clouds, except they're far bigger. Their base is well-defined and flat, but their upper edges are ragged due to the convection of air within the cloud itself.

Nimbus (Latin: "dark cloud") means precipitation is falling from the cloud. Cumulonimbus clouds are the "thunderheads" that can be seen on warm summer days and that can bring strong winds, thunderstorms, hail, and rain. They are fluffy and white like cumulus but are far larger. Their base can be up to five miles wide. At their low-altitude base, the clouds are mostly made of water droplets, but the high-altitude summits are dominated by ice crystals. Rain comes and goes with these clouds, and when it does, it can pour cats and dogs. When you see a cumulonimbus cloud, you can be sure there's a thunderstorm waiting in the wings. They are commonly seen during spring and summer afternoons, when the surface of the Earth releases more heat into the troposphere than at other times of the year.

Huckleberry Henry is well-aware that the next summer storm that comes pinwheeling out of the north might threaten the stability of his secret garden. His island in the sky is a piece of the Selkirks and a part of the main. If a few grains of granite be washed away by storms, he is the less, as well as if his entire plantation were. He is diminished by the wearing of the polished slabs in the cirques above No Telley Basin because he is intertwined with the 1.5-billion-year-old history of North Idaho. Therefore, he never thinks to send to know for whom the bell tolls, for he knows that it tolls for him, for all the friends of Priest Lake, and even for the lowlanders who only infrequently undertake the journey from the soggy pastures of their minds to the Jewel of North Idaho. (See John Donne, "Devotions").

When Henry looks up at the sky on a clear winter night, he unconsciously harnesses the power of Nature's incredibly detailed cosmological time machine. He is looking at the past. He traces the patterns of the constellations as they wheel across the sky, and his understanding of how Priest Lake formed 12,000 years ago is expanded to near infinite proportion. In a way, by embracing his immediate surroundings with a greater awareness of is relationship to the geological history of the Earth, and ultimately to the Cosmos, he is better able to reconcile time with eternity.

When Henry pauses in his nighttime travels to gaze up at the sky, he is looking back in time. The light arriving at his retinas comes from twinkling lights that are the farthest objects in the Milky Way. Some of it has been zipping across the Cosmos at 186,00 miles per second for tens of thousands of years. He sees the stars of our parent galaxy not as they really are, but only as they were long ago. And then, in awe of the city of God which has been shown to him, he shifts his focus to investigate the eternities, and by doing so, his observation is transformed to witness the future. With a greater appreciation of his mortality, he realizes that, in a sense, he needs the opposition of the past to serve as a counterpoint to the present, the contrast between the present and the future to experience his passage through time, and the ostensible finality of death to experience everlasting life. Only by discovering the terrestrial jewels that have been scattered about on the beaches of his life, will Henry recognize the diamonds in the sky that adorn the trail leading to a celestial city.

As Henry stares up at the night sky, taking in an aether that permeates God's Cosmos, it strikes him that each of us is a tiny universe within ourselves that contributes, in its own unique way, to a celestial community that manifests its armorial bearing with an overstatement that is truly galactic in scale.

Over the years, Henry has become Natures' Priest. When the rays of a hot August Sun beat down upon his sweating back, he doesn't take offense, nor does he pause in his labors. Instead, he finds it a cause for celebration. He rejoices that Mother Nature has noticed that he and his forest friends need Her nurturing influence, and that with just a beam of light, she can signal the grape arbor at his cabin to absorb heat from the Sun. His mountain home is transformed into a warm and inviting refuge from a cold forbidding world. As Emerson declared: "Give me health and a day, and I will make the pomp of emperors ridiculous."

Huckleberry Henry is not one to soon forget that symmetry, beauty, and proportion are the tools with which Nature has polished the gemstones that he has found scattered across the beaches of his life. His efforts to maintain their sparkle helps him to see beyond the veil that might have otherwise insulated him from the unreserved, unrestrained, unencumbered, uninhibited compassion of the Maker and Fashioner of the universe. Without the gemstones that have adorned his life, he might have forgone the knowledge and germination of faith, and have never embraced its fabric and its power to properly prepare him to choose the harder right, rather than the easier wrong. His faith has blessed him with focus, humility, and obedience; courage, endurance, and moral discipline, that he might more easily recognize the voice of God in the whistling wind and the rolling thunder, and in his mind hear a still small voice. These treasures are the only currency Henry needs to embrace a quiet sunrise or weather the storms of life, and to feel an abundance of His love in both circumstances.

Huckleberry Henry has lived boldly. With unflinching eyes, he has met the even gaze of Mother Nature. He has taken his place within a figurative shield wall, linked arm in arm with James Beckworth, John Coulter, David Thompson, Jeremiah Johnson, Bearclaw Chris Lapp, Del Gue, and others, and has stood his ground. When Mother Nature has thrown out the gauntlet, he has accepted Her challenges, aware that "to each of us upon this earth, death cometh soon or late. But how can we die better than facing fearful odds, for the ashes of our fathers and the temples of our gods?" (Thomas MacCauley, "Lay of Ancient Rome"). Henry has learned that it is a good day to die when, with the currency of his blood, sweat, toil, and tears, he has deposited grain after grain of sand upon the beaches of his life, until he has established a foundation, for it is on that solid ground that he will make his stand.

"Meet Joe Black" is a film that was loosely based on the 1934 motion picture "Death Takes a Holiday." At its conclusion, the protagonist, who is about to die, asks Death: "Should I be afraid?" When Death gently answers him and says: "Not a man like you," we know that, in the face of the inevitable, everything is going to be okay. When it's Huckleberry Henry's time to loosen his grip on mortality and reach out to touch the stars, we are confident that he will sense the warm embrace of heaven, and that he will be blessed with equally powerful reassurances of peace as he embarks upon that journey to an undiscovered country from whose bourne no traveler returns.

Stitched into the pages of the Lost Journal of Huckleberry Henry is more than a hint of an awareness of his mortality. In one entry, he speaks of ashes to ashes and dust to dust, suggesting his mindfulness of the inevitability of coming full circle. From time to time, he has cast simple glass jewels on the beaches between Huckleberry Bay and East Twin Island, but thru disproportion and the wear of constant abrasion, they have lost their luster. To him, the comparison is obvious, for he is painfully aware that, as the vicissitudes of life grind down upon him, his natural and native cheerful countenance could lose its luster, as well. He has tried to be an example to others of a rough stone rolling, and he hopes that the way he has handled his experiences might have restored the native sparkle to his naturally sunny disposition. His wish is that Priest Lake might exert the same transformative influence and return to gemstone quality the spirits of all those who come to inhale its aether. In the Selkirks, Henry has found what he was looking for; not just a gallon or two of huckleberries, but a life well spent. In the end, isn't that what we all seek?

Henry knows that in a coming day, he will hang his possibles bag on a peg by the front door of his cabin one last time. He will turn his back to No Telley Basin, effortlessly make his way up over Five Mile Ridge, and take the right fork of the trail leading to a banquet of consequences. With mouth-watering anticipation, he envisions his arrival at the festivities, where he will find music in the air and trees decorated with balloons and streamers, and serving tables crowded with venison roasts, squirrel stew, wild turkey breast, morel and chanterelle mushrooms, deviled duck eggs, crab apple pie and persimmon pudding, raspberry and elderberry tarts, day lily and wild asparagus, cattail shoots, carrot, garlic, and leeks, acorns and pinon nuts, sunflower seeds, and milkweed pods. But he knows that he will not find much that is satisfying, unless he is able to bow his head in reverence, and not hang it in shame, in the presence of His Maker, the Creator and Fashioner of the Cosmos, and of Nature Herself, the Queen Mother of all the Earth, who will jointly preside over the celebration as its Host and Hostess.

In anticipation of that joyful gathering, Henry has learned that he must begin now to adjust his internal chronometer to a celestial calibration. Priest Lake has had a mesmerizing influence on him; it has had a way of altering his perception of reality. As he has fallen under its wonderful spell, he recognizes that time is not a predator, after all. It has not been forever stalking him, but is instead a trusted traveling companion that reminds him to cherish every moment. Time is on his side as it gauges his approach to an event horizon beyond which lies the magic of an undiscovered country where fairy tales come true, and everyone lives happily ever after.

Epilogue

Huckleberry Henry has, on more than one occasion, encountered the ghosts of mountain men in the wilderness. Del Gue has been a persistent and infectious influence, exhorting him: "I ain't never seen 'em, but my common sense tells me that compared to the Selkirks, the Andes is foothills, and the Alps is for children to climb! These here mountains is God's finest sculpturings! In the Selkirks, there ain't no laws for the brave ones, and there ain't no asylums for the crazy ones! And there ain't no churches, except for the mountains, and there ain't no priests, excepting the birds. By God, I are a mountain man!"

Gue once told Henry: "Ain't what we got here somethin'? I told my mam and pap I were goin' to be a mountain man, and they acted like they'd been gut-shot. 'Make your life here,' they said. 'Here's where the peoples is. Them mountains is for Indians and wild men.' Mother Gue, says I, the Selkirks is the marrow of the world, and by God, I was right! Here, I can keep my nose in the wind and my eye along the skyline."

On one occasion, after a particularly long and hard winter, Gue counseled Henry "Maybe you best go down to a town and get outta these mountains." To which Henry responded, "I been to a town, Del."

Phil Hudson's Notes

I cannot take credit for this volume. The insights into wilderness survival, the historical
anecdotes, and the life lessons that are found within these pages belong to Huckleberry Henry.
It has been an honor for me to have been entrusted by Divine Providence with the care and
safekeeping of these entries that have been excerpted from his Lost Journal. I am humbled to have
been an instrument in bringing them into the light of day, that the sphere of his influence might
expand to include all those who love tramping in the woods below the Selkirk Crest. I feel that
I have gotten to know Henry as I have read his Journal, and I hope you will feel the same. I am
certain that he would be pleased to know that his thoughts have contributed to an appreciation of
the wilderness by so many of his friends at Priest Lake.

Henry's Reclusive Nature

Within these two volumes, many of their nearly six hundred illustrations depicting Huckleberry Henry were captured during chance encounters while I was hiking in the back country along the Selkirk Crest. Using a long telephoto lens with a tripod, most of the time he remained unaware that I was taking his photograph, although there were occasions when he seemed to be staring right into the camera. Henry has not explicitly given me his permission to include the graphics in this volume, but as the caretaker of his Lost Journal, and given the unusual circumstances under which it was found and has made its way to publication, I do not feel that their inclusion is a violation of his trust. It seems to me that the quality of the volume has been enhanced and Henry's story is better told because his edited journal entries include selected illustrations that are representative of his life. However, to protect his privacy, I have chosen not to divulge when, or where, or under what circumstances, the photos were taken. However, friends of Priest Lake may recognize in the background geographic features that could provide clues to the locations of Five Mile Ridge, No Telley Basin, the Woodland Elves' Glitter Mine, and Henry's cabin in the woods, that are frequently referenced in these anecdotes.

265

270

About Phil Hudson

Phil Hudson and his wife Jan have 7 children and 25 grandchildren. They enjoy spending time with their family at their cabin nestled in the Selkirk Mountains, on the shore of Priest Lake, the crown jewel of North Idaho. Phil had a successful dental practice in Spokane, Washington for 43 years, before retiring in 2015. He has an eclectic mix of hobbies and enjoys the out of doors. He always finds time, however, to record his thoughts on his laptop, and understands Isaac Asimov's response when he was asked: "If you knew that you had only 10 minutes left to live, what would you do?" He answered: "I'd type faster." Phil received the inspiration to write this book as he sat on the beach at Northwinds and looked out over the lake at the imposing skyline to the north, punctuated by Mollies' and Phoebes' Tips, Trapper Peak, Green Bonnet, and Little Snowy Top.

By Phil Hudson

A Broken Heart and a Contrite Spirit
Are Christians Mormon? (V. 1 - 2)
As I Think About The Savior
Baptism
Book of Mormon Hiking Song
Born In The Wilderness
Christmas Is The Season When…
Dentistry In The Scriptures
Discovering William Tyndale
Faith
Fitness Training For Mind and Spirit
Gratitude
Happy Birthday
Hebrew Poetry
Hiding In Plain Sight
Journey to Cumorah
Life's Greatest Questions
Mental Floss
Minute Musings (V. 1 - 3)

Muddy, Muddy
One Hundred Questions
Our Hearts Are Changed
Presents of Mind
Repentance
Revelation
Ripples on a Pond
Scriptural Symbols
Serendipitous Meanderings
Spray From the Ocean of Thought
That We Might Have His Spirit
The Atonement
The Hiawatha Trail: An Allegory
The Highways and Byways of Life
The Holy Ghost
The House of The Lord
The Little Princess
The Lost Journal of Huckleberry Henry
The Parable of The Pencil

The Plan of Salvation

This Do in Remembrance of Me

The Sabbath

Voices From The Dust

The Sacrament

Why We Are Baptized

The Strange Tale of Huckleberry Henry

Without The Book of Mormon

The Temple

Writing on Metal Plates

The Thirteen Articles of Faith

These, and other titles, may be purchased from online booksellers.

Index - Volume 1

If, when going through this Index, you find that you are prepared to elaborate on 25% of the listed subjects, you definitely qualify as a mountain man (or woman) and a true Priest Laker. If you score below 25%, read on, and you will soon have the knowledge to leave the ranks of those lowlanders who have never learned that, although the summit drives us, it is the climb that matters. Citius, Altius, Fortius!

Index - Volume 2

If, when going through this Index, you find that you are prepared to elaborate on 25% of the listed subjects, you definitely qualify as a mountain man (or woman) and a true Priest Laker. If you score below 25%, read on, and you will soon have the knowledge to leave the ranks of those lowlanders who have never learned that, although the summit drives us, it is the climb that matters. Citius, Altius, Fortius!

316

Publisher's Note

It is with pleasure that the publisher makes this announcement that great progress has been made relating to the discovery of additional authentic leather-bound copies of Huckleberry Henry's Lost Journal. If the clues that point to their location result in their discovery, the author has been given reassurances that at least one additional anthology, and perhaps more, will be green-lit for publication. In the meantime, please do not engage in pointless speculation relating to these further installments of Henry's Journal. Any announcements relating to the same will be made at the appropriate time, not on social media, but rather at one of the following expositions: the Frankfurt Book Fair, the Abu Dhabi Book Fair, BookExpo America, the Guadalajara International Book Fair, the Hong Kong Book Fair, the London Book Fair, or the New Delhi World Book Fair. However, it can be revealed at this time, that the entire series, whose working title is "The Lost Journals of Huckleberry Henry", has been projected by critics to be even more successful than the "Harry Potter" series with which you may be familiar, and which has sold over 500 million copies worldwide.